KILLING THE ANGEL OF DEATH

SPECIAL BONUS STORY "SPIRIT GUIDES"

KRISTINE KATHRYN RUSCH

WMG
PUBLISHING

ALSO BY KRISTINE KATHRYN RUSCH

CONTENTS

KILLING THE ANGEL OF DEATH

SPIRIT GUIDES

KILLING THE ANGEL OF DEATH

"I got another one." Rodrigo Jimenez sauntered through the uneven door into the tiny office.

Most people had to duck when they stepped inside. Rodrigo did not, and that always surprised Isadora. He looked like a much larger man—perfectly proportioned, almost square, with more muscles than she had ever seen on a human being before.

He stood just inside the canted doorway, his thumbs hooked on his back pockets and scanned the room as if seeing it for the first time.

She wished he wouldn't do that, because then she would see the room clearly too. Wax-coated paper coffee cups from the giant 1980s hot beverage machine in the shared hallway toppled out of the plastic garbage container near the door. The recycling bin was mostly empty, just a few circulars and advertising flyers that Rodrigo would toss in there whenever he came into the office first.

The pilled beige industrial carpet needed vacuuming

(needed replacing, really), and an inch of dust covered the windowsill in front of the half-open window.

The dust wasn't Izzy's fault. The office was in a strip mall on a very busy road, and if the window was open, the entire place filled with road grit within fifteen minutes.

Still, the place was a sty. He knew it, and she knew it. He wanted it to be shipshape at all times; she didn't care. She figured the person who cared the most should be the person to do the work; he figured everyone should be cleanly.

That was only one of their many differences.

"We have enough people," she said, not moving from behind the faux wood oversized desk they had found at a warehouse that specialized in cleaning out old offices. At least she had a modern chair—her back didn't accommodate the green-and-steel concoction from the 1960s that Rodrigo had picked up at the same warehouse.

"We don't and you know it." Rodrigo flopped on the ratty brown couch—her furniture contribution—and folded his hands behind his head. "We need a sniper."

"I don't like guns," Izzy said for the five-thousandth time.

"Then leave the damn project," Rodrigo responded, as he had each time. It had become a ritual. They had to get through the *I don't like guns* routine before they could have a real discussion.

"You can shoot," she said.

"I'm not accurate at long distances." He tilted his head slightly. "That's a special skill."

She supposed she knew that. She supposed she knew lots of things. But most of that knowledge came from television. With Rodrigo, most of his knowledge came from life.

"You're stalling," he said. "You just don't want to go the Meeting."

She rolled her eyes. "God, the fucking Meeting." She hated the Meeting. Everyone there had eyeballed her weird the day she had given her "testimony," and the "facilitator" had had the balls to tell her that maybe she needed to find a meeting outside the city, in a place where people would understand her grief.

She had never even gotten to her grief. She had started wrong, started with the trigger—Bongo's death. She'd told them how losing her only friend had started a downward spiral, how she had actually stood in front of her medicine cabinet and stared at the contents inside, how the fact that he hadn't wound his furry feline way around her legs in that moment of crisis made the moment of crisis even worse.

She'd come back, though, because Rodrigo—whom she hadn't known at the time—had touched her arm.

"These people," he said, "they don't get it. Some of us do."

And then he'd left. And because of that moment of compassion, she'd returned one more time, and had to endure some scrawny kid shaking his head and whispering loudly to the dumpy middle-aged man beside him, "Oh, God. The cat lady returns."

Rodrigo had saved her. He had shut the kid down with one steely look, then brought Izzy a coffee from the burned mess in the scratched gray urn at the back of the room.

She clutched the cup he'd brought her and listened to tales of grief clearly more harrowing than hers. The dumpy guy, watching his wife die by inches after she was burned in a fire; the scrawny kid, losing his best friend in a freak accident at a water theme park.

Most people didn't speak, though. They listened, picked

at their clothing, watched the clock on the wall, and drank too much terrible coffee. The "facilitator," a thin nervous woman who seemed to prefer faded print dresses three sizes too big, mouthed the platitudes Izzy had expected: *Grief is a process. We all experience it differently. It's different with every death. Ride the waves and understand that this, too, will pass.*

If Izzy wanted platitudes, she would have gone to church. She had figured that something that billed itself as a Grief Support Group, held in a half-forgotten side room of City Memorial Hospital, would actually be run by someone with credentials, someone who understood grieving, someone who actually cared.

It seemed like the only person who had cared had been Rodrigo, and except for talking to her that first day, and bringing her the coffee on the second, he hadn't said a word. He just sat near the back wall, wooden chair tilted back, massive arms crossed, and watched the proceeding as if he were the body guard, not someone whose life had been upended by death.

She later discovered that *upended* wasn't even the right term. The last ten years of Rodrigo's life had been all about death, and he was trying to find a way to deal with it.

Or he had, before the shooting.

"It's not even the same Meeting," he said, as if to placate her.

"It's always the same Meeting," she said and made a face.

The new Meeting was more of an offshoot, and could more accurately be described as a Survivors' Club. Yeah, they welcomed new members, but usually those people left when they realized the group was *that group.*

That group was the one that had—according to the media —failed so badly at providing support that one of the members hauled out an automatic rifle and slaughtered everyone in the room.

The truth was different, of course. No one had been in the room when Dugan had entered from a side door. The Meeting had ended. Half the group was standing on the sidewalk in front of the door. A few had already left, and two or three more were in the parking lot, on the way to their cars.

Rodrigo was close to the door, smoking a cigarette—illegally, since state law proclaimed that he had to be at least ten feet away. He saw Dugan barge out, swinging the rifle wildly, and Rodrigo said (not that anyone would listen) that Dugan wasn't in his eyes.

Rodrigo had seen PTSD, hell, Rodrigo *had* PTSD, and he knew when someone was flashing back, and he was convinced (not that he had any proof) that Dugan was back in whatever war zone his trauma had come from. Dugan had only described the events once—something about a group of guys arriving on a truck in a dusty village, swinging rifles, picking off everyone around them, and he had been sharing a meal with a friend, and he couldn't get his weapon out or didn't have the right weapon or something.

Anyway, Dugan walked with a limp, had a scar that ran up his entire left side, and more guilt than any man should have.

He had come out of the side door and picked off six people on the sidewalk before heading toward the parking lot, tripping on the curb, falling on his hands and knees, the rifle skittering away. He ran his fingers along the concrete, said something like, "Oh, Jesus, no," and that was when the first cop arriving on the scene had shot him.

Rodrigo hadn't had a weapon, or he'd have shot Dugan too, but not a shoot-to-kill. Something that would've let the man live long enough to explain himself, maybe long enough to feel regret.

Rodrigo had tried to stop Dugan. Rodrigo had been halfway to the parking lot when the cop wheeled up and fired out of the driver's side window. That was when Rodrigo—whose skin was darker than Dugan's—hit the deck.

Izzy knew this part of the story, because Rodrigo had told her. She had given up on the Meeting by then, given up on being called The Cat Lady, given up on the "facilitator," who had been shot in the shoulder and wrist, but who had survived. That "facilitator," whom Izzy couldn't stop thinking of as a job with air quotes, had never come back.

The hospital's insurance company paid for everyone's medical care, but refused to let any more grief meetings take place onsite without a trained psychiatrist running them. The hospital didn't have any trained psychiatrists it could "waste" on people who were "merely" grieving, so the Meeting moved to its current location, and the survivors acted as facilitators, rather like an Alcoholics Anonymous group.

Not optimal, but at least honest. And much as Izzy hated the Meeting, she still showed up sometimes and stood in the back, just because she kept hoping something would fill the hole inside her.

Or maybe she just wanted to see how everyone was faring. Grief piled on grief piled on grief led to breakdowns. She had no idea how much the trauma of a shooting added to the stress, but she figured it couldn't be considered minor.

She hadn't even been there, and she thought about it every single time she passed the old meeting site. She wouldn't even park in that wide-open parking lot, because there was a stain near the curb. Rodrigo said it was an oil stain, but she didn't think so. Three people had bled out there, and somehow that blood got absorbed into the cheap asphalt.

She firmly believed that places got haunted by the violent dead, and the hauntings always took a form that was recognizable by the survivors.

She counted herself a survivor, even though she hadn't liked most of the people who had died.

Now the Meeting was held about a half mile from the

office, not near any hospital at all. The space was in the basement of an ancient Y. The Meeting shared the large room with AA, Adult Children of Alcoholics, Narcotics Anonymous, and Gamblers Anonymous. The weekly meeting schedule was posted in different colors for the different groups, plus there were flyers, and some poor kid who volunteered at the Y maintained the meeting schedule on the Y's creaky old website.

It was all too complicated for Izzy or, at least, that was what she told Rodrigo. He never missed a Meeting. He was more facilitator than the old "facilitator" had been, and he actually seemed to care about the others.

Which made his cooperation with Izzy all the more surprising.

He walked to the Meeting. She drove, because she wanted to be able to escape without waiting for him.

Her car was an ancient Mustang which had once been a new Mustang, her husband's pride and joy. Her husband was long gone—everywhere except in her guarded heart. His presence wasn't even part of this Mustang any longer.

He would have hated the way the leather bucket seats had tiny tears along the base, the garbage piled up behind the front passenger seat, and the fact that the Bose Sound System he'd lovingly put in by hand now couldn't play a cassette tape if she even owned one to play. The black exterior hadn't been washed in more than a year—the last time the day some kid had scrawled *Wash Your Fucking Car, Bitch, Or Lose It* in the dirt on the rear window.

She parked, like she always did, five rows down, where the parking lot had buckled and weeds as old as the Mustang had grown out of the cracks.

She had passed Rodrigo about three blocks away,

charging forward because the man never walked slowly. She meandered across the parking lot in the mid-afternoon heat, wondering why she stayed in the city when the summers were torture and the winters were worse.

Then she stopped two doors down from the side entry to the Y, and watched people enter, trying to guess which one of them was the one that Rodrigo wanted her to see.

"You won't see her until you get inside."

As usual, Rodrigo had snuck up on Izzy. No matter how hard the man charged, he still moved like the Seal he had been a lifetime ago.

She didn't start, though, when he spoke to her, although her heart had sped up just a little. She had been prepared for him to come up behind her, and she had still been surprised when he spoke.

"A woman," Izzy said, glad she sounded calm. "I didn't expect that."

"You think women can't be snipers?" he asked, but didn't wait for her answer. Instead he walked to the door and pulled it open.

It was one of those heavy metal doors with a barred grill just above eye level—at least for her. The scents of sweat, chlorine, and fifty-year-old coffee wafted out at her.

The Meeting had been held here long enough now that she had begun to associate those smells with despair.

She stepped inside, blinking in the sudden darkness. It took a moment for her eyes to adjust.

This door opened into the old lobby. The new lobby was two floors up, and actually looked inviting. This one still had the Formica desk sticking out of the wall, the cubbyholes in the back that used to house mail and keys for the residents who lived upstairs, and a few chairs, crowded around the scratched window that opened over the pool.

The pool was also in the basement, but on a different side from the meeting rooms. The window didn't keep a lot of the sound out. Kids screamed and laughed. Something boomed and splashed, and a lifeguard yelled.

The pool was uncomfortably close to the meeting rooms in the basement. They were all damp and smelled of both mildew and chlorine. There were no windows at all in any of the basement meeting rooms, single exits grandfathered in by virtue of the fact this building had stood in the same place since the 1930s.

The pool had been revamped in the 1970s, and at that point, someone had slapped cheap paneling all over the basement, but the paneling only made the rooms darker and the smell of mildew stronger.

She followed Rodrigo down the curving staircase behind the old desk, feet slapping against the metal stairs. The railing had rusted years ago, and hadn't been replaced. She always wondered if the damn thing would hold her up if she needed to catch it in a fall.

She doubted it.

But she doubted a lot of things.

At the base of the stairs, a confusing catchall area was the only place she ever saw anyone who swam. They'd come out of the locker room, hair wet, some kind of duffel over their shoulders, and gaze at her with bleary red eyes, wonder why an overweight woman with silver lining her hair was even anywhere near an athletic facility.

They never looked at Rodrigo that way. They looked at him like they expected him to order them back into the pool, then make them swim fifty laps before they thought of leaving again.

Doors veered off in five different directions, something she'd found very confusing the first few times she had come here. Now she knew they had to take Door Number Three (not marked that way—it wasn't marked at all. It was just the third door from the base of the stairs).

Above her, the florescent light buzzed and blinked, making her feel slightly dizzy. *Stay in this area too long*, her brain warned like it always did, *and we're going to give you the worst headache of your life.*

Rodrigo pushed Door Number Three open, and headed into the narrow hallway that contained three rather tiny bathrooms (of the male, female, and handicapped variety) and two different doors on opposite sides that led into the same damn meeting room.

It was the smallest room in the basement, and Izzy was convinced it had once been some kind of storeroom. Three florescent lights hid inside plastic panels on the ceiling, panels that lied and claimed there should have been six lights.

The ubiquitous back table held three of the Y's black beverage urns—one for coffee, one for hot water and one, weirdly, for hot cocoa, even in the summer. Donuts from one of the morning meetings hardened on a platter near the cocoa urn. Clearly the morning meeting hadn't been Narcotics Anonymous because those folks always cleared out the sugar, even if it was crap sugar like those donuts.

Someone had put out the folding chairs in five rows of seven with an aisle in between, and a podium up front, causing Rodrigo to swear. Half the group, including the scrawny kid, were gathered near the coffee urn. Of course none of them could bother to set up the room properly.

Rodrigo slung the chairs into a circle like they'd been made of putty. It wasn't until Izzy start to help him that she realized one chair was occupied. A woman sat in the back corner, farthest from the door, out of view of the podium, and nowhere near the snacks table. She blended into the darkness as if she was made of it.

Izzy knew without Rodrigo saying a word that this was the woman he'd brought. Not because the woman had wrapped herself in darkness, not because she was good at remaining in the shadows, not even because she exuded an air of *fuck with me at your peril.*

It was because she was angry.

So furious in fact that the air around her felt like it had been charged with violence.

The last thing this group needed was another violent angry person who couldn't deal with whatever had happened to her. The group ostracized folks this obviously angry—had since Dugan decided his anger was more important than their lives.

Most angry grievers, they'd leave after the first meeting or two, but it was clear this woman had been here before. She didn't seem alarmed by Rodrigo, knew who to hide from, and actually had a question in her eyes when she saw Izzy.

The woman had been here enough to know that Izzy wasn't a regular. No five times per week whether she needed it or not for Izzy. More like once every five weeks whether Rodrigo could drag her here or not.

"Need the chair," Izzy said.

The woman didn't move. "Looks like you got more than

enough."

That was true. Thirty-five chairs and only ten people near the coffee urn, twelve if you counted Izzy and Rodrigo. Thirty-five was the hopeful number they'd promised the Y when they took the space; thirty-five was the fiction they maintained even though the Meeting hadn't hosted more than twenty since the massacre.

"Still," Izzy said, "you shouldn't sit in the back."

"And you shouldn't come once in a blue moon and think that entitles you to giving people orders," the woman said.

"Iz," Rodrigo said. "Sit."

As if she were a misbehaving puppy. As if she would respond to orders at all.

To prove her independence or her contrariness or her orneriness, Izzy went to the other table, the one with stick-on name tags and blue magic markers, scrawled *Isadora* on one that cheerfully proclaimed

Hi! I'm _____!

She was half-tempted to add a smiley face with sharp pointy teeth after the second exclamation point, but figured that would only show her age, not help anyone understand her attitude.

She slapped the nametag on her shirt, hoping she would remember to remove the damn thing before someone on the outside grinned and pointed and said, *Isadora, huh? That's an unusual name.*

She didn't even get coffee because she wasn't going to stay long enough. She had a hunch she'd bolt in the middle of the first story. She was feeling itchy already.

But she sat in the chair Rodrigo had indicated, which

was—not coincidentally—directly across from Hidey Woman. Izzy couldn't even see the woman's face in the shadows, just her scuffed Nikes and her bare ankles peeking out from a pair of pristine blue jeans.

From the pool area, the life guard's whistle cut through the low murmur of conversation. Last warning or clear the pool or Ready Set Go. Izzy never knew which it was, but she always found it amusing that this version of the Meeting started with a prompt from a *life*guard.

The world was full of ironies and this was one of them.

The group took their chairs, balancing coffee, some cookies she hadn't seen, and next week's schedule, clutched in nervous fingers. She recognized all the faces—the dumpy guy, who'd lost half his body weight after the surgery to remove a bullet from his spleen; the fat lady, mother of five full-term stillborn babies, who, like Izzy, hadn't been at the Meeting that day of the shooting; and the scrawny kid, who gave Izzy the evil eye, as if everything bad that happened in the world was somehow her fault.

Rodrigo didn't start the meeting. He rarely did. That afternoon, the honor fell on Clarabell, a wizened seventy-something who claimed she'd been named for a stupid clown on a stupid kid's TV show.

That's how my childhood played out, she'd said bitterly one afternoon before the shooting. *Imagine what that was like, particularly when it was clear to everyone but me that the obnoxious clown was male.*

Back then, she'd gotten sympathy from the Meeting—before the scrawny kid and the dumpy guy and their judgmental attitudes had shown up. Now, she never mentioned it and, Izzy noted, she no longer wrote *Clarabell* on her nametag. Now it simply said *Clara,* as if that made every-thing better.

"It's been five months," Clarabell said. "How's everyone holding up?"

No hellos, no *let's introduce ourselves,* no discussion of where and what the meeting was. Not even a mention of what she was referring to. If there were any newcomers here—and Izzy didn't think there were except maybe Hidey Woman—they were on their own when it came to under-standing just what the hell was going on here.

"Just a reminder," said a bearded man near the door. "The hospital's insurance only pays for six months. If you want to continue therapy after that, you'll need a referral."

"And insurance of your own," the dumpy guy murmured.

"Fat fucking chance of that," the scrawny kid said.

"We've got each other, anyway," Clarabell said, but she didn't sound too sure of that. What did they have, really? A shared room in the dank basement of an old Y, an experi-ence that bound them together in group tragedy, after they'd come together for comfort from personal tragedy.

That was about all Izzy could take. She bounded out of her chair, only to have Rodrigo grab her right arm and pull her down again.

He leaned over to her. "You're listening this time," he whispered.

Her stomach knotted. "She talk at all?" Izzy asked, nodding at the woman.

"Not yet," he whispered. "Maybe not ever."

"Then I'm leaving." Izzy shook off his hand, and stood again, saw the scrawny kid glaring at her, and knew what he would say if he felt like he could—like he used to before the shoot.

What happened, Cat Lady? Need to get home to kitty-kitty-kitty?

Fuck you, she sent him, as if telepathy were real. *Fuck you and your superior fucking attitude.*

Yeah, she still had anger issues. One year in, and she was beginning to believe that the wheel of grief wasn't a wheel at all, but a gauge with her needle stuck at *Fuck You Forever You Fucking Asshole.*

Or as Rodrigo liked to delicately call it, *The anger phase.*

Izzy pushed her way out, back to the narrow hallway, the strange little room of doors, the buzzing florescent, and the scuffed staircase. The smell of chlorine made her sneeze.

She was really tired, the kind of tired you got when every day was a burden, and every hour seemed to last longer than the one before it.

She glanced up the stairs like they were her enemy. Rodrigo had said the woman wouldn't enter by conventional means, which meant she wouldn't leave by conventional means either, and Rodrigo wanted Izzy to meet her.

Izzy could go back to the office, and wait, only to have Rodrigo bawl her out, and then drag her to yet another Meeting on yet another too-hot afternoon.

Or she could sit on the stairs and brood until the Meeting ended. One hour, if the schedule was to be believed. Because a half hour after this meeting ended, the Wednesday AA group would saunter in for their discussions of twelve steps, compulsions, and higher powers.

No one ever talked about higher powers in the grief groups that Izzy had attended. Higher powers were there to help with addiction, not with loss.

All she knew was that any time someone murmured *It*

was God's will at the Meeting before the shooting, someone else would snap something rude about God.

It was Rodrigo's response that Izzy had never been able to get out of her head.

If that was God's will, he'd said, referring to something he had never really told the Meeting in detail, *then God is a goddamn motherfucking son of a whore sadist, and I hope to Christ I never meet the motherfucker face to face.*

Rodrigo's outburst had silenced the room. No one had seen him lose it like that before, and maybe not since.

Izzy had, but Izzy talked to him outside of the Meeting. Izzy knew that her anger was nothing compared to his and there were days when he felt a kinship with Dugan. *Sometimes,* Rodrigo said more than once, *it'd be a lot easier to blame someone for the whole mess.*

Why? she'd asked only once.

Because then I'd take the motherfucker out, he said, his voice so cold and chill and flat that she had no doubt he'd do it.

No doubt he'd find a way.

And she had held onto that for the six months before the shooting and four months beyond. The month of the shooting, she'd half blamed Rodrigo. If he'd been that close to everything, how come he couldn't stop Dugan? Dugan had taken out the one person that Izzy had liked at the Meeting, a sixteen-year-old girl whose baby sister had died of leukemia.

What had those parents done to deserve that response from God? They lost both their children—one to a disease that had a 90% survival rate for most kids, and the other to something stupid and random that had happened because she'd been trying to take care of herself, trying to move forward with a life that should have extended eighty or more years ahead of her.

Izzy tried not to think of Alyssa because it only pissed her off. Alyssa—no tats, one piercing in each ear, and only a slight hint of pink over her dark brown hair, straight As, and the ability to cry without moving her face.

She was the only one of the group who haunted Izzy, maybe because she had been the only one who had ever touched Izzy's heart.

The door banged open, and conversation filled the hallway beyond Door Number Three. Izzy stood, brushed off the back of her jeans, and leaned against the rusted railing, trying to look cool rather than distraught—not that anyone would notice.

Just her luck that scrawny kid would come out first. His skin was clearing up. He'd also gotten taller in the past few months, but his eyes were still sad.

She leaned toward something like compassion for him when he reached her.

"You know," he said, "the Meeting actually works better when you sit through it."

He didn't wait for her response. He bounded up the stairs two at a time, and disappeared before anyone else came through the door.

Apparently, the Meeting had bothered him too.

Izzy moved away from the stairs after that, taking refuge near the door to the women's locker room. No one else noticed her. She counted bodies as they left...seven... eight...nine with scrawny kid. Which meant that Rodrigo was still inside the room with Clarabell.

He could handle himself, but sometimes it was polite to rescue a friend, even if that friend had dragged you unwillingly to a meeting you really never wanted to attend.

Izzy sighed and pushed off the wall, heading into Door Number Three, listening for conversation as she went. Nothing. Which meant that either the door was still closed or they weren't talking or something else was going on.

Her stomach clenched, because it always clenched when something out of the ordinary happened around the Meeting. But she made herself ignore the feeling.

She opened the door, and as she did, the snap and slam of metal folding chairs being flattened grated her. Rodrigo was gathering the chairs, closing them with one hand and then adding them to the pile he managed to carry with the other.

At first glance, he seemed to be alone in the room. No Clarabell, no stragglers hanging out by the coffee.

Then Izzy saw the Hidey Woman stacking another set of chairs in the corner. That surprised Izzy. She figured Hidey Woman for someone who dwelt in the darkness and never helped anyone in the light.

"Isadora," Rodrigo said, as he added one more chair to his impossible arm pile. "Thought we'd lost you."

She wasn't sure if she should let Hidey Woman know just how vulnerable Izzy really was.

"Waited outside," she said. "Meeting go okay?"

"The Meeting never goes 'okay.'" Rodrigo was very good at spoken air quotes. "But we got through it."

That, she wanted to say to him, *was not a recommendation.* But she bit the words back because she also didn't want to discourage Hidey Woman from attending.

Izzy believed that if someone found the Meeting valuable, they should not be discouraged from attending.

Rodrigo took his impossible pile of chairs over to the Hidey Woman. Apparently his strong arms had reached their limit. He handed her the chairs as if they'd been at this routine for a while.

"We've got about ten minutes, Iz," Rodrigo said.

It wasn't so much a statement as a command. *Get your ass over here. If we're going to talk to her, we're doing it now.*

Izzy nodded, then walked across the room, almost stopping for coffee just so she would have something to do with her hands.

She reached Rodrigo and the Hidey Woman as they put the last two chairs into the pile. The room looked so much bigger when it was empty.

"Isadora, meet Lana." Rodrigo said.

Lana. The name didn't quite fit her. Too mundane, too short, too bland. The Hidey Woman—Lana—didn't move, seeming to wait to see what Izzy would do.

Izzy held out her hand. "Izzy. I prefer Izzy. Rodrigo likes the formal name."

Lana didn't nod. For a brief second, Izzy thought Lana wasn't even going to extend her hand for a shake, and then she did, slowly and languidly, resulting in one of those rich lady handshakes: *I'm too wealthy and pampered to bother to squeeze her hand. In another life, I would have hand you courtesy and kiss my ring.*

The attitude, the thought, and the shake that inspired it surprised Izzy. She'd expected a firm, masculine grip, something tough as tough could be. Rodrigo had said *sniper,* after all.

But Lana was tiny, and didn't seem to be any kind of sniper at all. She barely came up to Izzy's shoulder, but stood with the perfect posture that spoke of early (and

22

intense) ballerina training. There was a set to her head, the way her feet seemed to prefer a modified version of second position, the precision in her movements.

Her hair was long and pulled into a bun, her dark eyes dominating her small face, and her chin was narrow, giving her face a startled foxlike appearance.

Not threatening at all.

But, then, people thought that about Izzy too.

"I thought we could talk to Lana about what we do," Rodrigo said.

Izzy looked at him. His chocolate brown eyes peered down at her with the full expectation that *she* would talk to Lana about what they were *planning* to do, since as of yet, they hadn't done anything.

There was no good way to start this conversation. Start with an apology, and Izzy would be at a disadvantage. Start with a question, and she gave Lana a chance to back out. Start in the middle of it, and Izzy would sound like a crazy person.

She chose a fourth option.

"You ever hear of the Angel of Death?" she asked. "We're going to take him out."

3

The reactions were always predictable. Some people backed away. Others laughed nervously. A couple said, *Wouldn't that be nice.* And one or two—the ones that stuck—didn't say a word.

They simply waited for more information.

Lana's gaze never left Izzy's. Waiting. Withholding judgment until the very end.

"We're building a team," Izzy said. "Rodrigo believes you could be part of it."

Izzy deliberately left herself out of that statement. She didn't know enough about this woman, didn't know enough about what this woman could do. Wasn't even sure Lana was as billed.

Until Izzy remembered that air of violence, the one that had accompanied Lana in those shadows, making her seem bigger than she actually was.

"The Angel of Death," Lana said quietly. "You believe that is a real being?"

There it was: the loss of control of the conversation. And

to make things worse, she answered a question with a question.

Izzy gave Rodrigo a sideways glance. He nodded, almost imperceptibly.

"You know there is," Izzy said, deciding to be somewhat aggressive. "If you didn't, Rodrigo wouldn't have brought me here."

Lana looked at him, as if seeing him for the first time. Then she brought that measuring gaze to Izzy.

"If there were such a creature," Lana said, "then it would be immortal and untouchable. Going after it would be a fool's errand. Even if you could kill it, something would replace it, and death would simply continue."

"You don't use death to stop death," Izzy said. "You use death to get revenge."

"'Vengeance is mine, saith the Lord,'" Lana said.

"If that were true," Rodrigo said, "all of human history would be very, very different."

Lana's eyes narrowed, and she smiled, tilting her head to the right as if conceding a point.

Her entire body relaxed just enough to be noticeable.

"You want to send a message," she said.

"I do," Rodrigo said. "I absolutely fucking do."

4

They didn't ask her if she believed in the Angel of Death. She had asked them. Lana had done her best not to seem incredulous. She had tested them with the Biblical quote, because religious nuts often went off the deep end about the angel of death or the destroying angel or whatever Christianity called it.

Every religion had a personification of death, maybe to make it real. And each personification was different.

Just like each experience with the so-called Angel of Death was different. She firmly believed in those beings in the light people who had been brought back from the dead had seen. They hadn't been benign actors, beloved people from a former life. They had been death angels, deciding which fish to keep and which ones to throw back.

The death angels never really had a plan, she thought. More like a desire to see what would happen this time if they screwed with a particular person.

"I'm in," Lana said quietly. "I'm definitely in."

5

The first time she had seen what they were calling the Angel of Death, she'd been six. She had been eating dinner at the kitchen table with her sisters, her parents, and her baby brother, still in his high chair. The room smelled of mushy peas and beef gravy, a radio played Madonna's "Vogue" in the background, and the grownups were talking about something Lana didn't understand. Then, the light in the room dimmed.

She looked up, saw a person, indistinct and shadowy, with his fingers wrapped around her father's throat.

Therapists later asked why she thought the person was male. She couldn't articulate it then; she could now. Male hands looked different from female hands. Just slightly: a little broader. A little flatter.

Or maybe, she sometimes thought, the hands had been familiar. Hands she had seen a lot as a young child, hands of a person she no longer remembered.

But she remembered that moment. Those hands, squeezing her father's throat. He continued talking, as if nothing was wrong, as if the knuckles on those hands around his throat weren't turning white with effort, as if the life wasn't being choked out of him, bit by bit.

"Mommy," she had said, terrified. "Someone's hurting Daddy."

Her mother had looked sideways, her own face indistinct in the memory, as if Lana had no words, no reference for the expression on her mother's face.

"I'm fine, honey," her father had said to her, his voice as calm as ever. "I'm just fine."

And then he had stood, put his fingers on the kitchen table for balance, and toppled sideways—someone—and she never knew who—catching him and easing him to the ground.

Of course, at that moment, he had already been dead.

Family lore said that Lana claimed someone had hurt her father after he had already fallen. But her mother always watched her with a bit of speculation, as if worried that Lana might tell *her* that someone was hurting her, and then her mother would die.

Her mother hadn't died yet, at least that Lana knew about. She hadn't seen or spoken with her mother in more than a decade.

There simply was no point.

They had nothing in common. The Bible that Lana could quote with ease was her mother's beloved book, not hers. Lana didn't have a religion. She wasn't an atheist. She believed there were things in the world that she did not understand.

But she also believed that they were unknowable, and that religions simply guessed, trying to make people feel better about their miserable little lives.

She had never thought of her life as miserable or little, not until recently. She couldn't shake the images, the fear, the guilt.

The anger.

And she had come to believe that people didn't die of old age; they died of an accumulation of death—dead parents, dead children, dead friends. At some point the accumulation defeated them, and they succumbed.

She could feel her accumulation pressing on her. Some people—they had low death tolerance. Others had a higher one, like a high pain tolerance. They could handle so much more than most people could

She was one of those, she had thought. But lately, she hadn't been.

It was the accumulation. Friends, colleagues, enemies. Victims, too, since she had killed her share, always at the direction of her government, for something she had once believed in, something she was beginning to think had been perverted, if it had ever truly existed at all.

6

They took her to a dumpy office in a dying strip mall. Rodrigo and Izzy seemed at home here, with the 1970s wood paneling, the beige carpet that probably hadn't been cleaned since 1990, the couch that looked older than Lana.

She had expected something sparkly, something that spoke of magic, not something that looked as defeated as she felt.

They promised her pizza while they waited for the rest of the team. The pizza arrived first, which was probably good, considering that the team was much larger than she expected. The ham and pineapple pizza was mostly demolished when the first of more than a dozen people came through the hollow-core fake wood door.

She missed most of the names, mostly because the people pouring in weren't what she expected.

She expected more soldiers like her and Rodrigo. Or police. Or mercenaries. People with skills she knew and understood.

And there were maybe some of those—maybe seven, if

she could judge by posture alone. But those weren't the folks who caught her eye. They passed by her as if they were partially invisible.

She was watching the gorgeous drag queen in a flowing pink pantsuit and glittery heels who had clearly dressed down for the afternoon. Then Lana noticed the young person who wore black jeans, a black shirt, had dyed his (her?) hair shoe-polish black like Joan Jett used to wear hers, wore black lipstick and black eyeliner, and had painted her (his?) fingernails black.

He (She?) was followed by another person whose gender was deliberately ambiguous, a slouchy thin person who wore a knitted hat despite the heat, a hoodie with a picture of kittens and chainsaws across the front, and jeans that had more holes than material.

Two twenty-somethings came in next. The twenty-somethings looked like teens, until Lana saw their faces full on. Prematurely lined, even though neither young man had reached his full growth. Their dark faces had the texture of hard leather, the kind of faces people who suffered from too much sun exposure usually got in their forties.

They barely acknowledged her as they flopped on the filthy carpet.

Behind them came a rotund woman who looked like she should have fronted a cable baking program from the 1980s, a scrawny elderly man with hollow eyes, and an ethereal girl who appeared to be no more than twelve.

The girl's eyes were dark, and, at this distance appeared to be without pupils. When Lana turned away, movement caught Lana's eye again, and for a half second, she thought she saw wings.

But when she looked at the girl directly once again, the

girl looked like a normal twelve-year-old, long-limbs and flat torso, with the promise of beauty to come.

Not everyone came from the Meeting, as Rodrigo called it. Some Izzy had found; the others Rodrigo brought. The drag queen invited herself, after her gender-neutral friends had found the place—by accident, they claimed, although Lana was beginning to think there were no accidents here. The drag queen, in turn, had invited two thin, sad-faced men who sat in the back with their arms wrapped around each other, almost for protection.

There appeared to be more men than women which surprised Lana, and the women were less athletic than she would have expected. Three of them looked like teachers or librarians or some other cliché of middle age.

Several African-Americans, and one Asian-American woman who looked tougher than everyone else put together. Everyone younger than thirty appeared to be mixed race, although with the makeup on the kid wearing all black, she couldn't really tell.

Lana took a can of Diet Pepsi, and retreated to a corner, leaning against the wall, the handgun she had a concealed carry permit for pressing against the small of her back. She always wore loose shirts to cover it, not that anyone ever noticed the gun or her. Although here, everyone saw her anyway, which was a brand-new experience for her.

She had spent so many years practicing the art of invisibility that she had no idea what to do when she was actually being seen.

"They're here to vet you," Rodrigo said, but didn't explain how they would accomplish that.

People found their places on the floor, leaning against the walls, and sitting on the handful of chairs. Some folks had brought coffee, others drank bottles of water they had brought with them. The two twenty-somethings each took a piece of pizza, then waved them at the others, as if asking permission to eat.

No one complained, not even Lana whose appetite had left her.

Izzy sat behind the desk, half hidden behind a slender PC that appeared to be the newest thing in the place. Rodrigo rested one thigh on the desk, bracing himself with his other foot.

Just like he was at the Meeting, he was the leader here without saying a word. He waited until everyone settled, and silence grew—except for the rattling of an air conditioner that had been old when this place was built.

Rodrigo studied the faces around him, then glanced at Lana.

"I think we might've found our sniper," he said.

She started. She had never told him what she had done. She had left it all behind, the shootings, the kill orders, even the rifles. She hadn't held a weapon in three years.

Correction: she hadn't *actually* held a *real* weapon in three years. Every time she fell asleep, she woke up to find her left hand braced underneath her rifle, her eyes pressed against the scope, her trigger finger at the ready.

That there was no rifle didn't really matter. There had been one. And, apparently, it would always be with her.

And, apparently, it would always be visible to sensitive folks.

Or folks who had done a boatload of research.

Although she wasn't sure how he could have researched her. Lana wasn't the name she had been given by her religious mother. Lana was the name she had chosen, picking that name only because it was easy to spell, easy to remember, and unusual enough in this day and age to make it feel like hers.

Rodrigo was watching her watch everyone else, which made her nervous. After the group had settled, she did an actual count.

Fifteen, not counting herself, Izzy, and Rodrigo.

Fifteen people who had somehow, for some reason, decided they needed to take out the Angel of Death.

Lana let out a small snort at the thought, felt a half-smile start, and made it stop before it became a full smile.

No one besides Rodrigo was looking at her now, and then she realized that wasn't true. One of the semi-invisible librarian women was staring at her, and so was the drag queen.

The drag queen, clearly over six feet tall, made taller by the heels in her glittery sandals, walked over to Lana, extended a manicured hand, and said, "Starina."

Lana raised her eyebrows, and said, "Really? You took on the name that Nathan Lane's Albert used for *his* drag queen in *The Birdcage?* Really?"

The drag queen let her hand fall. "Sarcastic and all-seeing. What did you find for us, Rodrigo?"

"Snipers are great observers," he said quietly. "And we don't need names. This is not the Meeting."

"I'd say welcome, honey," the drag queen said, emphasizing *honey,* "but I'm not sure about you yet."

Lana wasn't sure about any of them. She sipped her Diet Pepsi, trying not to wince at the fake-sugar aftertaste, and then watched them watch her.

"If we're going to stare silently at each other," Izzy said from behind the computer, "I'm going to go insane. So, one word or one sentence, name your last straw. We'll end with you."

She didn't say Lana's name, just glanced at her so that Lana knew who *you* meant.

"I'll start," Izzy said. "Cat."

She said it defiantly, as if challenging anyone to laugh at her. Lana wasn't sure she understood what Izzy was even asking for, given the cryptic nature of the one word and the command.

"Nephew," said one of the women sitting on the floor.

"Roadside bomb," said the military man next to her.

"Traffic stop," said the man beside him.

"Judy's," said the thin man with his arm around the other man. The other man nodded, and said, "Judy's."

That, at least, Lana recognized. Judy's nightclub shooting, October of 2016, in the middle of the presidential campaign from hell, everyone thinking that maybe the rhetoric from the Republican nominee (and the local candidates) inspired three shooters to kill twenty people and wound sixteen more, just one town over.

Lana had loved Judy's. Big-hearted, with a beautiful painting of Judy Garland in all of her incarnations adorning the wall that the police eventually shattered with big rescue vehicles they'd gotten because of 9/11 funding.

She expected the gender-neutral kid in all black to say Judy's too, but he (she?) said, "Faghole," and a teenage girl near him nodded. Lana knew the insult too. Instead of "asshole," "faghole" was something mean homophobic kids had started shouting at kids whom they found different. But she didn't know it was a place or a thing or something that would cause a vision of the Angel of Death.

The rounds continued.

"Best friend."

"Fucking cancer."

"Emergency room," said one of the librarian women. "Night after goddamn night."

So not a librarian. A nurse.

"Judy's."

"Fifteen-car pile-up."

"Traffic stop." Again. She didn't quite see who had spoken.

"The neighborhood, man," said one of the men on the other side of the room. "Just the freakin' neighborhood."

"Judy's."

The ethereal girl shook her head, waving her hand, as if she still couldn't speak about whatever it had been.

"Hot truck abandoned in the desert," said one of the leathery young men. The man next to him nodded.

The nearest desert was two thousand miles. But deserts, Lana got deserts. Deserts. They were deadly.

"My son," said one of the muscular men, whom Lana had pegged as a cop.

"Portage Elementary," said the man next to him.

The school shooting—the worst kind of school shooting (as if there were any good ones)—two states over. First-graders. Who the fuck killed first-graders?

At least two assholes in the United States had done so.

Two.

Spurred on by the Angel of Death.

Lana set down her Diet Pepsi, brought her knees to her chest, and hugged them.

The voices around her were dry, matter-of-fact, listing more family members, more friends, more circumstances.

The litany got to the drag queen, and Lana braced

herself for another *Judy's*. Instead, the drag queen said, "Pepperbeans," and the beefy man next to her patted her hand, and gave her a sympathetic smile before he said, "The best grandmother in the entire world."

It took less than five minutes for the litany to reach Lana. She glanced at Rodrigo, who was staring at her. He hadn't said anything, just like the ethereal girl and one of the librarian women.

But no one mentioned that. No one urged them on.

Yet everyone stared at Lana as if she could give them her entire life story in one word. Last straw. They thought there was a last straw.

"You assume there's just one," she said quietly. Her voice wasn't as flat as she wanted it to be. She wanted to sound as matter-of-fact as they all had, and she couldn't.

She just couldn't.

She didn't belong here.

She pushed against the wall, then made herself stand. They all watched her.

"It's silly anyway, right?" she asked, "talking about death as if it's something we can attack, something we can stop."

The woman who hadn't spoken, the one who hadn't given a reason for being there, stepped in front of two of the other librarian-looking women. This woman was about fifty pounds overweight, but she carried it well. Her face had been sharp and angular once, but now there was extra flesh under her chin, a slight puffiness to her eyes.

Her hair was iron-lady gray, and she didn't wear any makeup at all. But she was wearing a dress, and not a sundress either. Something that pretended to be businesslike—or would have been forty years ago, when they didn't make suits for women.

"You were hoping for something magical," the woman said, her voice soft. She had a slight Southern accent, but from what state, Lana couldn't tell.

Lana wanted to deny the accusation, but she remembered her disappointment when she had seen the office, how she had wanted something sparkly, something that didn't look defeated.

But everything seemed defeated here—and she knew, they *all* had to know—there was no magic in defeat.

"Something…Disney," the woman continued. "Something…over the top."

Tears pricked at Lana's eyes. So what if she wanted that? So what if she had hoped for a little magic in her life? So what if she had thought maybe she would find it here?

"You make the mistake everyone makes when they think of magic," the woman said. "You think it's easy. It's not. We don't do easy here."

"What do you do?" Lana let the defensiveness out. "Sit around and plan revenge on something that doesn't even exist?"

The woman looked at Rodrigo, who shrugged one shoulder.

"You deny that death exists?" the woman asked Lana.

Lana let out a bitter laugh. "If only."

"Then stay. Listen. Assess when we're done."

"Let her go," one of the men said. He was one of the men she had taken for a cop, although his last straw had been something like the death of a parent or something. "We got enough shooters."

"Not long-range precision shooters," Rodrigo said. Then he looked at Lana, as if he was disappointed in her.

She stood even straighter, and measured the distance between her spot on the far wall, and the door.

"Snipers," he said, "usually don't join something like this."

"We're not joiners," she said.

"No," he said. "That's not it. Snipers usually think of themselves as the Angel of Death. They don't need someone to remind them that there is another mechanism in place, something that can kill without a scope and ammunition."

Her cheeks heated. "I'm not that arrogant."

"Oh, but you are," he said. "Or you would not have taken the job of sniper."

"I tested into it," she said. "Best shot in Basic. Best shot in every single unit I joined. They finally recruited me."

"And you let yourself be recruited," Rodrigo said.

The blood left her cheeks, taking the heat with it. "I don't 'let' myself do anything," she said. "I took the job."

"Why?" he asked.

They were all staring at her. Had she taken it because she was arrogant? Because she liked killing?

"Because there was no one better," she said, her fingers clenching into fists. "Because, there was *no one* better."

7

Jubilee had had enough. She watched the sniper woman step into the center of the room, small and powerful, her body in perfect shape, each motion made with great confidence. Jubilee had not been that confident at that age. In fact, she had only become confident when she had become her true self, a process that had taken forever.

Half the people in the room caught Jubilee's movement, and waited quietly. Her friends from Judy's, they knew that Jubilee could be tough when she needed to.

But she hadn't needed to in this group. She had let Rodrigo run everything, let Izzy handle all the details, figuring they were the organizing type.

Jubilee had other things to do, other things to think about.

But she didn't feel that way now. This group was much more important to her than she realized.

For one of the few times in her recent life, she wished she had worn something less dramatic, something less pink. She had seen that little sniper woman dismiss her, simply because she was wearing clothes that made her comfortable, clothes that made her feel stronger, and for some reason, she wanted the little sniper woman to respect her.

Jubilee would never learn.

That very thought had gone through her head when she introduced herself to the sniper woman as Starina. Jubilee had been poking, figuring a military woman with a tough background wouldn't respect her from the start.

Jubilee had been surprised that the sniper woman had known the reference, and had been even more surprised when the sniper woman had called her out about it.

Jubilee had just been developing a little trust in the sniper woman when she went all *This is a bunch of hooey* on them.

Jubilee stood. Tru clutched at Jubilee's arm, trying to stop her. Tru and their good friend Mica usually had a finger on the temperature of the room. But Jubilee didn't want a temperature. Jubilee wanted to make a point.

"Let her go," Jubilee said, nodding at the sniper woman. "She's made it clear that she doesn't want to participate. We don't need to convince anyone to be part of our group. People need to convince us that they belong."

She raised her chin ever so slightly, her voice shaking more than she expected. She hadn't thought she would be so passionate about who was on the team.

But she was.

Because this was important.

No matter what the sniper woman thought.

8

It had taken Jubilee years to find someone who had seen the same things she had. Not in the world—God knew anyone who was grew up queer or different experienced the same hatreds, the same prejudices.

It was those little fleeting glimpses of something else, something on the edges. Not just when someone died. But when someone hated. When someone harmed. When someone lied.

The first time she'd seen it, she hadn't even known Jubilee was inside her. Then she'd been Dennis, the kid who hunched over and hid most of the time. Dennis had been too tall, too "effeminate" in the words of her gym teacher, who had literally tried to knock "some sense" into her three weeks into the fall semester.

High school in Wyoming, where men were men, and Matthew Shepard had been beaten, tied to a fencepost, and left to die like a tiny 5'2" human scarecrow only two years before. Jubilee had met a lot of great people, compassionate people, in Wyoming, but none of them had understood the cost of growing up different in a small Western town unless they had experienced the same things.

Coach had tried to make Jubilee a basketball star. Anyone that tall needed to be playing basketball, that was Coach's thinking—ignoring Jubilee's lack of interest as well as a lack of physical coordination that came from a 10-inch growth spurt that had happened over the space of one short summer.

The tauntings, the beatings, the way some of the boys tried to catch her alone, to show her exactly what was waiting for her if she didn't toughen up, a reality all of her life, until she'd discovered some like-minded folk in (ironically) Laramie, who actually showed her how to deflect, how to avoid, how to protect herself.

Still didn't stop her from getting stomped that night in March, beaten within an inch of her life. She had been laying on the slushy concrete, her right cheek half-frozen against the ice, hot blood dripping down her face from her shattered nose, eyes half open, staring at Andrew as he died just across the parking lot from her—Andrew, the only person who had ever been kind to her. Andrew, who was not gay, was not trans, was not anything except the nicest human being in the entire world, killed because he had dared—*dared*—to befriend the wrong person.

That night, something had flashed underneath the streetlight, just before Andrew had died. Wings, maybe. A face, rather like Oz's big see-through head floating above the flames in the movie *The Wizard of Oz*. (Maybe that was one reason Jubilee idolized Judy. That moment when she faced down the Wizard. It was not just everything Judy had done, everything she stood for—but her courage, her desire to defend everyone, including a scarecrow who was smarter than anyone and more vulnerable than everyone knew.)

That night, on the ice, bleeding out, Jubilee (Dennis then) had stared at the wings under the street light. The wings got smaller, the face faded, and then there was the smell of vanilla, almost overpowering, and a touch of snow. She had the sense that the creature had just come from Andrew, that it had been (feeding?) on Andrew, and now that Andrew was no more—eyes empty, body unmoving— the thing had flown to her.

She hadn't been sure that was bad, not at that moment, with her whole life ahead of her filled with, as far as she could tell (as far as Dennis could tell) more beatings, more hatred, more loss.

Then something caressed Jubilee's face, feathers—or so it seemed—soft and soothing. And the smell of vanilla had grown a lot stronger. At least she liked vanilla. Vanilla suggested warmth to her, maybe even love.

Then, suddenly, she heard voices across the parking lot, voices that made her shiver or maybe just made her realize how helpless she was, broken against the pavement. She waggled her fingers, tried to move her feet—why, she'd never know, because she had no idea if those voices belonged to the boys who had beaten her and killed Andrew, or if the voices belonged to someone who might consider rescuing her.

One of the voices said, *There's another one,* and came closer, and she cringed. The smell of vanilla had disappeared, the feeling of warmth, the feathers on her face, replaced only by the crusty edges of blood around her nose, the throbbing in her shattered left cheek, her left eye, slowly swelling shut.

The voices belonged to people who had no idea who she was (what she was), thought she was just some boy who'd gotten beat up, and then they found Andrew too, and they thought mugging gone wrong, so they called the police, called an ambulance, and somehow, some way, Dennis survived.

Andrew was dead, but Dennis hung on for a few more years. Hung on to what Jubilee never knew, because the depression after that, the waves of despair, they grew and grew and grew.

And Dennis almost faded away.

Somehow she got out of Wyoming. Scholarships—at least education saved her, more or less. When you hid and studied you actually got somewhere.

For her, somewhere was NYU, New York, with all its variety, and she found like-minded people, she found people who saw *her*, not Dennis, and brought out *her*, brought Jubilee into the world, and showed her how to be herself. She entered a community that meant so much more to her than any other community ever had, graduated from college with a degree and a real job, where people didn't care who she was as long as she met the unisex dress code (she could do that), and for a moment—just a moment—she thought the world would treat her well.

Then she watched, watched, watched as friend after friend died. Some old timers, finally succumbing to the opportunistic diseases that took advantage of someone HIV-positive, others dying the same way Andrew had— from fists and bigotry and too fucking much hate.

By the time Jubilee had transferred here for work, she was strong. She was Jubilee. She was numb.

She knew the back passages of Judy's, and she knew how

to recognize the Angel of Death. The Angel didn't have wings this time—sometimes the Angel had wings and sometimes it didn't. Sometimes it looked like a man, and sometimes it looked like a woman—rather like Jubilee at one point in her life. Sometimes it looked human and sometimes it looked like a clichéd demon. And sometimes, sometimes, it took the form of a lover or a loved one or souls who had passed and—she thought (they all thought)—would never return.

Only once had the Angel tried to impersonate Andrew. Only once. He had come toward her in the midst of her despair—one of those dark nights of the soul that not everyone climbed out of. She'd been beaten—again—in a parking lot—again—by assholes—again. But she'd learned those details much much later.

What she remembered, what had been real to her, was that feeling, that *Why the fuck am I bothering? Nothing ever changes.* She was twenty-five, out of college, still in New York, but in the wrong part of the city for a concert, and she'd dressed like Jubilee. Her mistake, even though they said that the victim should never consider their clothing a mistake, but she did, she had, and she felt—oh, God, she felt like *what was the goddamn point?*

The Fake-Andrew-Angel had reached for her just as she had thought *Maybe I'll let go this time,* and the Fake-Andrew-Angel had smiled at her. It extended its hands—which looked like Andrew's hands—and for a moment, she was fooled, thinking maybe it was Andrew, maybe there were good people where she was going, a different kind of life there, one that wasn't so painful.

Then the Angel's fingers brushed her face, like feathers, and it said, *Jubilee, Jubilee, it's been too long. Love, I've missed you*—and the words were so wrong, the sentiment so far off, that she knew, *she knew*, this wasn't Andrew. Not her Andrew, not the only person who had gotten her through that hellish high school. Not the person who had died defending her.

Had died defending Dennis.

So as the Angel put its Fake-Andrew fingers on her face, Jubilee slapped them away. Then she had punched it in the jaw.

The thing was, she had never punched anyone before. Not once, in her entire battered life. She'd been the punched. She'd never been the puncher. She usually curled into a fetal ball. She had stopped begging that night in high school, in that frozen parking lot where Andrew had died, because she'd learned then that begging only made things worse.

Her punch, though. Her punch had been involuntary, filled with a rage she had never before acknowledged that she had. Fake-Andrew-Angel had staggered backwards, surprised, hand on its cheek, its eyes black and all pupil for just a moment, wings flaring around it as if it planned to fly off.

Then it dropped its hands, and said in Andrew's plaintive voice, *I thought we were friends.*

Andrew and I were friends, Jubilee had said. *You pollute his memory. Get away from me.*

And the Angel left. Just left, as if it had been a vampire in a movie and she had thrown holy water on it.

Everything around her cleared. She wasn't in some magical realm. She wasn't even somewhere warm. She was in another parking lot, one she had not ever seen before.

Her torso underneath a dumpster that stank even

though it was nearly zero degrees outside. Her knees and toes were numb—exposed to the cold because she was wearing the open-toed shoes she preferred at her favorite club—and her entire body ached.

The dumpster—it was a sign. Someone (smaller, not as strong) had tried to toss her in it. That someone had failed.

She never remembered the fight—not that it was a fight. It wasn't fair to call a beat-down a fight, and she never knew who attacked her, although she could guess why.

She couldn't remember anything from the evening leading up to the dumpster. The only thing she could remember was Andrew-Fake-Andrew the not-so-fake angel, and knew, at that moment, that she had tangled with something bigger than herself.

The ambulance that had arrived just as she had woken up out of that trance (was that why she had awakened? Because an ambulance had arrived? Because someone had tried to save her?) managed to get her on a gurney before she even knew what was happening. And then one of the attendants said that phrase that she had heard only once before in her life: *Wow,* one of the attendants said, *you'd think someone who had been through all that would be dead.*

Then he saw her looking at him through a rapidly swelling eye, and he winked at her. Not a sexy wink, but the wink of someone who knew and understood.

You're lucky, honey. You made it out this time, he had said. And that *honey* had been a gift, not an insult. Just a bit of understanding on a horrid horrid night, a night that should have ended everything.

The next morning, every part of her ached, except the bruised and battered knuckles on her right hand. Those bruises, the doctor said, looked more like electrical burns, but they didn't act like burns. They were clearly bruises that resembled the kind of burns Jubilee would have gotten if she had stuck her hand in an electrical socket and the socket had exploded.

That was how she had known the punch had been real, the surprise had been real, the Fake-Andrew-Angel had been real.

A therapist told her, later, that she had seen things, but they hadn't been real. They had simply been the electrical impulses of an oxygen-starved brain.

Science, the therapist had intoned, *has shown that most of these near-death visions are simply synapses firing in unusual ways because of the stresses on the body.*

But the knuckles? The bruising? The black streaks, which had remained for the better part of a year?

No one had answers for that. No one except Jubilee who, at that moment, decided to believe.

She'd even asked the therapist, taunted the therapist really, in the last hour they ever spent together, the last hour Jubilee ever paid for.

What caused these marks, then? Jubilee had asked.

The therapist shrugged. The person who was supposed to have all the answers *shrugged,* and said, *Your body simply chose to express the trauma in that way. Bodies do that.*

Jubilee hadn't believed that at all, although she found it curious that the therapist, who was part of the community, had seen marks like that before, had thought those marks somehow normal. Now, Jubilee would want to ask the therapist about it, but then Jubilee had simply felt rage.

The therapist had gotten a concerned look, folded her hands together, and intoned to Jubilee: *Respect the trauma, and you will eventually heal from it.*

Respect the trauma. Jubilee actually heard that part. Respect the trauma. Realize that something had happened to you. Something big, something profound. Something difficult.

Respect the trauma had become her mantra. And it got her through.

It got her through breakups and the deaths of friends. It got her through the loss of her soul-mother, the woman who made it possible for her to become Jubilee in the first place.

It got her through that night at Judy's.

She had been in her dressing room, getting ready to go onstage. She'd been performing at Judy's three nights per week. She'd been bartending on three other nights. The job that had brought her here was long gone.

That night, she'd heard gunfire, and it sounded close. She never know why she had grabbed three feather boas, and some extra-large panty hose at that moment, but she had. She burst out of her dressing room, pointed at the scared young stagehand, and told him in her most commanding voice to call 911. Which he did as she went to the doors that separated backstage from the gunfire, and she had locked them, tying the feather boas in place for added strength, protecting her backstage crew while they tried to escape out the exit doors.

At that point no one—not the shooters, not Jubilee—had thought about the stage as a way to get backstage. All she had done was think about the doors, barricading the doors.

There'd been three shooters that night, not one. The media couldn't decide if the deaths at Judy's had been an act of terrorism, an act of hatred, or an act of some local deranged minds, rather like the attack on Jubilee and Andrew all those years ago.

Jubilee knew it had been all three—she hated that term *domestic terrorism*—but that's what it was. Bigotry mixed with deranged minds, mixed with easy availability to weapons, and some sick reason to attack people who were only out to have a good time.

She'd gotten twenty people out, before one of the shooters broke through the doors she had locked. She kicked off her heels—not sure why she hadn't kicked them off before, but adrenalin, panic, had caused her to make some strange choices—and then she had climbed the catwalk as quietly as a 6'2" person could. Fortunately, she hadn't put on her costume. She was wearing her bra and Spanks, her real hair which she kept short so she wouldn't get too hot under her wigs, and her feet were bare now. Bare, making climbing easier, if painful.

She'd reached the top of the catwalk, and she'd dumped one of the lights downward, narrowly missing another one of the shooters, the one standing on stage, firing into the audience huddled on the floor. Later, she found out, he had been hit with shards of broken metal and glass. At least she had caused the motherfucker some pain.

He whirled, pointed his rifle upward, and shot God knows how many repeating rounds. Missing her as if she were Tom Cruise in every single movie he'd been in. The shooter ran as he shot, shouting at his compatriots that she was here, there was someone above them, someone else who had to die.

She'd seen the wings again that night, but not the Fake-Andrew-Angel. Instead, he had come to her—*it* had come to her—as her beloved soul-mother, sitting on the edge of the catwalk.

You know it would be less painful if you fell, her fake soul-mother had said, so far off target again, that Jubilee's breath caught. Whoever this so-called angel was, it was bad at its job. Or maybe it hadn't done its research or maybe it was simply supposed to confuse.

Instead, it had goaded her, just like it had the first time. Only this time, Jubilee jostled the catwalk, then kicked out with her bare feet, catching the fake soul-mother angel-asshole off guard, and it toppled headfirst toward the stage.

Its wings unfurled at the last second, but not soon enough to do anything except ease the fall. It landed with an ungainly thud and a cry of pain that everyone in the club seemed to hear, including the cops, who were, at that moment, shooting their way in.

Adding to the casualties of course. Because police in minority communities always added to casualties.

That was something she'd tried to impress on the four police officers on the team Rodrigo had put together, but those police officers still didn't understand it, not even the African-American one. They talked about triage and the need to save some if you couldn't save all, and she always argued that you had to save all, until she realized that arguing was futile. There were simply some things even reasonable people, even reasonable people with something in common, simply could not agree on.

No one shot her that night at Judy's. Somehow, she got out. She managed to find friends, reunite lovers, get phones to those who needed to call family *right now.* Someone gave her a coat, and someone found her some shoes, and still she worked, tirelessly, calmly, making sure everyone in her community was A-Okay.

The local papers started calling her the Angel of Judy's until she made them stop. Because she'd seen the angel at Judy's and it hadn't been one she wanted to emulate.

She'd been fine after that—no need for therapy, not her, not this time. She had finally (she thought) found her calling, the ability to hold friends, friend-family, and acquaintances together, to keep a damaged and grieving community alive. To be the rock in the center of chaos, the one everyone went to when they needed a shoulder, when they needed a hug or a good meal or just someone to sit quietly in the same room, listening to each other breathe.

And then Pepperbeans died.

Pepperbeans, her little long-haired white mutt of a dog. Pepperbeans hadn't been at the club that night, although Pepperbeans usually went everywhere with her.

But Jubilee had received a few death threats, ones she believed (she didn't always believe the threats), and when she believed a threat, she knew it was better to leave Pepperbeans at home, because sickos who targeted the LGBTQ community targeted animals too. Bigots always saw dogs as easy prey and Jubilee hadn't wanted to lose hers because Pepperbeans had had the misfortune to be at the wrong place at the wrong time.

Pepperbeans, fourteen years old, getting a little creaky, but not anything else. The dog loved her treats. She loved playing with Jubilee, and she loved cuddling at night—a warm little snuggle that had become reassurance after all the darkness.

Until the snuggle ceased to be warm.

Pepperbeans had died three weeks after Judy's. Perfect

death, really. The kind that Jubilee would want if she got a vote in how she passed away. In her sleep, at home, snuggled against her favorite person in the whole wide world.

The vet said it had been quick and it had been natural causes, and no, Pepperbeans hadn't suffered at all. *If you have to pick a way to go,* the vet said, echoing Jubilee's thoughts, *then this is absolutely the best way.*

Not that it helped Jubilee. She beat herself up internally worse than any of the beatings she had gotten for being different. What had she missed? How could she have saved her dog? Why couldn't she save her dog?

And why—oh, God, why—did Pepperbeans have to leave now?

The despair threatened to eat her alive. Jubilee knew the despair wasn't all Pepperbeans. It wasn't even close to Pepperbeans. Izzy's words "the last straw" were accurate, if a bit minimizing. Pepperbeans simply stood for all the loses, all the deaths, the one last factor that nearly tipped Jubilee over the edge.

Until she remembered that she had punched one version of the Angel of Death, and shoved another version off a catwalk. What would she have done if she had seen the one that had come for Pepperbeans?

Would Jubilee have recognized it? Was there a dog version of the Angel of Death? Was it something she could have stopped?

And those thoughts brought the recriminations back all over again.

She clung to the recriminations even as she tried to find a way to make them stop. She played with them in her mind, over and over and over again, as she rebuilt Judy's, as she held friends, as she still provided comfort.

She even looked at other dogs, but couldn't—just couldn't face loving another one, loving something good and small and innocent. Not when she was surrounded by so much death.

And it had been that thought, that very thought, which had come to her in, of all places, a no-kill shelter, that she was surrounded by death, even in places like this, which had banned it.

She could see the Angel of Death. And if she could see that motherfucker, she could hurt it. She could hurt it bad.

Once she did that, once she scared it like she had scared that one near the dumpster, she could demand that it change its ways. It could still do its job. People who got horribly ill, with no hope of recovery ever, just misery forever, they needed some kind of respite. And, if she were honest with herself, she didn't mind if the angel killed a few homophobes, a couple of terrorists, and a mass murderer or two.

But Pepperbeans, who had simply loved her? Andrew, the best person in the whole world? Her soul-mother, who taught Jubilee that we all had someone special inside us; we simply had to find her?

The Angel of Death shouldn't get to take the good ones. No one should take the good ones. No one at all.

Stalking sounded easier than it was. Jubilee probably could've staked out nursing homes or the ICU at the hospital, maybe followed some hospice nurse on her daily rounds, but that didn't just seem fair. That seemed wrong.

If she went to visit the dying, she should actually give them her time and her full attention, not scout around to see if some stupid "angel" approached on little death wings.

She had been sitting in a park—a dog park, honestly,

because she missed having a dog. She watched other people's dogs frolic on the somewhat matted and stinky grass, and thought about stalking (and fucking destroying) the Angel of Death.

Only she didn't know how to go about it.

Then Rodrigo sat down beside her.

She hadn't known him then, hadn't known he was a good and kind person, hadn't known he gave as much (if not more) of himself than she gave of herself. All she saw was a squat muscular man glancing at her from the corner of his eye.

She was taller than he was, but obviously not tougher. She knew a man like him could take her down with two quick moves—had taken her down like that more than once.

Her heart started beating rapidly, and she gathered her purse, her book bag, and her coat.

"Stay," he'd said.

She gave him one of those dismissive smiles, the kind she'd learned from the woman who'd been her soul-mother. So many deflecting things Jubilee had learned, the way women blew off men without ever really confronting them.

She nearly dropped her purse, that was what kept her on that bench a half-second longer, grabbing the purse strap, mentally cursing, thinking about everything she could have done but wasn't doing and—to be honest—wondering why the hell she couldn't even get a moment of peace, when he spoke again.

"I want to kill him too."

She looked at Rodrigo in complete horror. He wasn't looking at her. Instead, he was staring at a little brown shih tzu that stood in front of him, tail wagging happily, and for a moment, Jubilee thought he had been talking about the dog.

"You see him," Rodrigo said. "I know you do."

She froze in place. Surely, he wasn't there. Surely, he wasn't talking to her. She had been leaning forward just a bit to gather her things, and she leaned just a bit more and, in a not-as-surreptitious-as-she-would-like kinda way—she looked to see if he was on his cell, if he was talking to someone else.

Of course he wasn't. He was talking to her.

He had meant it all for her.

Then he looked at her head-on. His eyes were brown, and they seemed kind. She hated it when the people who attacked her initially seemed kind. Things like that made her already-fragile belief in humanity become even thinner.

"Every time," Rodrigo said, "I see a man. He looks like a soldier out of uniform. Straight back, khakis, sleeves rolled up to reveal powerful arms. His face is wrong, though—not quite human, an approximation of human— or maybe we're all that kind of approximation when we're killing."

That phrase, that sentence, it made her shiver. Was he threatening her? She pulled her purse up by its strap, hugged it to her. The shih tzu barked playfully, and leapt back and forth, trying to get Rodrigo's attention again. Instead, another dog showed up, a bigger dog—some kind of mutt—and they ran off together, playing and barking with great joy, exactly the way the park should work.

Rodrigo must have seen her expression (how could he miss it, after all?) and he smiled ever so faintly. "I didn't mean to alarm you."

Talk of killing, talk of *death*, with a stranger, and he hadn't meant to *alarm* her?

Her coat was caught between her left thigh and the rusted metal armrest. She couldn't quite get free.

"Five tours," he said. "I kept reupping. I don't know why. Guess I thought I could make it better."

She froze again, heart still pounding, but somehow willing to listen. How did he continue to find that sweet spot, the one that kept her just barely in place, unwillingly hanging on his every word?

"You see him," Rodrigo said again. "I *know* you see him."

And this time, he sounded just a little desperate, as if he didn't want to believe he had made a mistake sitting next to her, a mistake engaging in conversation with her, a mistake revealing so much about himself.

Revealing what, though? That he was just a little crazy? Or maybe not a little crazy. Maybe a lotta crazy.

She'd learned long ago not to engage with crazy. She managed to free her coat. She slung her purse over her arm, and stood up in one single movement.

But she couldn't help herself. She had to say something. She was going to say that she didn't think he should talk like that to strangers.

Instead, she told him something she'd learned in the community damn near her very first week in New York.

"Pronouns are important," she said. "It's not a 'him.' It's an 'it,' no matter how it presents itself. It's an it."

He rocked backwards as if she had pushed him against the bench. Then he tilted his head just a little, nodded, and smiled, as if her words had clarified something for him.

"What do you see?" he asked quietly.

"People I knew," she said bitterly. "Misappropriated images of people I knew. And wings. And it smells like vanilla. Put me off ice cream and vanilla lattes for the rest of my life, let me tell you."

He gave her a second smile, but it looked perfunctory, as if he knew her comment required one.

Then he patted the bench.

"Sit back down," he said. "Let's talk."

She didn't sit. She was never going to sit because some muscular man told her to.

He glanced at the bench, then shrugged just a little, as if to say that it didn't matter if she sat. It would be her loss to continue standing.

"There are people like you," he said, "like me. People who see him—it. Who see it."

In spite of herself, she appreciated the correction. He was trying. She wasn't sure she wanted him to try, but he was.

"It..." he seemed to be searching for the word. "It changes us."

"Death changes us," she said, shifting her purse on her shoulder. Dogs barked behind her, and a tall Doberman entered the park as if he and his person owned it.

Rodrigo inclined his head, giving her that point. Then he said, "I mean, when we see him...it. When we see it, we become different. We think of it as something..."

Again, he seemed to cast about for the word. But this time, he couldn't seem to find it.

"Something we can fight," she said.

His gaze flattened for a moment, as if that hadn't been the word he had been searching for. Then he sighed, and shook his head once.

"I was going to say we want to fight it, but that is wrong," he said. "Except for the deeply ill and those who die in an instant, we always fight death."

"And suicides," she said softly.

"Deeply ill," he repeated, and she bristled. She did not believe suicide was an illness. Sometimes, it was a choice in the face of great physical pain. Or in the face of a world gone mad.

Or maybe she simply felt insulted by the comment, considering all the times she had considered suicide, and then (mentally) walked away from it.

"Then," he said, apparently not seeing evidence of her own internal dialogue, "I was going to say we want to defeat it, but that is not right either. Because much of our science, our medicine, our psychotherapy and religion, it is all about defeating death."

"I suppose," Jubilee said, suddenly tiring of the conversation. He was getting philosophical with her, and she didn't enjoy that. Apparently, he was borderline crazy after all.

He sensed it. He could sense her mood changes. Perhaps they showed on her face.

"I finally realized," he said quietly, "that the word I want is *stop*. We want to *stop* death. Entirely."

"I don't," she said coldly, shifting her coat to her other arm. "There are some people who deserve to die."

And then she walked away from him, threading her way through the dogs, her heart getting heavier and heavier each time one planted itself in front of her, with a doggy smile on its face, tongue lolling, tail wagging.

She nearly made it to the edge of the park, when she had to go back.

He was still sitting on the bench, staring at the dogs as if they held all the answers.

"Why did you talk to me?" she asked as she approached. "What made you say all that stuff to me?"

He peered at her, almost as if he had forgotten her. Then his brow furrowed, and he took a deep breath—a man who was unwilling to speak, after talking so very much.

"Because I can see it," he said quietly. "On your right hand. You touched one."

Then he ran his fingers along the back of his own right hand, exactly in the place the black marks had been on her hand.

It unnerved her, but this time, she didn't want to step away.

"I didn't touch one," she said. "I *punched* one."

Hard. Hard enough to startle it. Hard enough to make it have second thoughts even as it tried again.

"Punched it," he said quietly, and then he chuckled. *"Punched* it."

He shook his head, and his smile grew with each shake. He was incredulous and yet somehow joyful, and the look transformed his face, from something broad and tough to something almost handsome.

"Punched it," he repeated.

She felt a smile building inside her. It did sound ridiculous, Jubilee, punching the Angel of Death.

"And I kicked one," she said. "Hard enough to make it fall."

He raised his head, his gaze meeting hers, and his smile, which was already broad, grew into a gigantic grin.

"You've fought the Angel of Death twice," he said.

"If only I'd won," she said.

"Oh, you did," he said. "You're still here."

"For the moment," she said, not willing to promise anything more than that. "I'm here, for the moment."

Somehow, he convinced her to have coffee. Then coffee became lunch, and lunch became dinner, and the conversations went on into the night. The people they'd known, the people they'd lost.

She shared more than he did, but she always shared more than anyone else, so she didn't think it unusual until much later, after she had joined the group and watched him with others.

They all talked about their last straws and their broken hearts and the day when everything changed for them, but he rarely said a word. He watched instead.

She had no idea what his magic was, but she knew he did have magic. It was subtle and hard to see, but it showed up, like it had when he spotted her, like it had when he ran his fingers along the back of his right hand in the same pattern as her black marks.

When he "saw" something, she learned to pay attention, although she didn't always approve.

And she didn't approve right now, of this woman, this sniper that Rodrigo seemed to think they needed.

They hadn't even decided on weapons yet. Jubilee wasn't even certain that weapons would work. They didn't even have a true game plan, just a series of ideas, wishful thinking all of it, nothing concrete. She wasn't sure they would ever have anything concrete. She wasn't even sure concrete was possible.

And yet she was offended when the sniper woman—incongruously called Lana—stood up and declared their mission silly. Even though part of Jubilee agreed. Part of her knew that death had always been a part of life. So many ancient cultures believed—taught—told everyone—that without death, life had no meaning.

Jubilee wasn't sure she believed that. She wasn't sure she wanted to believe it. She wanted to think that life could be as precious, as fleetingly perfect, without the ever-present threat of an ending looming in the distance.

The sniper woman was staring at her. Jubilee couldn't tell if she saw disgust in the sniper woman's eyes or if the sniper woman always looked at everyone with great contempt.

Perhaps it was the sniper woman's defense mechanism. Or perhaps the sniper woman was truly as arrogant as she had sounded just a moment before, when she declared herself the best shot in her unit, the best shot in any unit she had ever belonged in, implying that she was also the best shot in any unit she *might* find herself belonging to.

"Let her go," Jubilee repeated. "We don't need attitude like that."

Usually, when Jubilee spoke here, in this office, everyone listened and agreed. This afternoon, they listened, but no one nodded. They seemed uncertain, as if they were at a crossroads none of them completely understood.

"She stays," Rodrigo said, without looking at Jubilee.

"If she wants to," Izzy added softly, her gaze on the sniper woman.

The sniper woman turned her gaze from Izzy to Rodrigo, and then back to Jubilee.

"What are you people going to do if I try to leave?" the sniper woman asked. "Kill me?"

Tru let out a guffaw. Jubilee looked over at Tru.

"Dude," Tru said, as only they could do, putting the emphasis on *dude* in such a way as to make even that word seem slightly ironic. "We're here to stop death. Dude. I mean really. We would kill you because you won't help us stop death? How dumb is that?"

The sniper woman leaned back ever so slightly, her cheeks turning a slight shade of pink. Apparently, she hadn't been put in her place in a while.

"What do you need a sniper for?" the sniper woman asked, without the edge of her earlier comments. "I mean, if there is an Angel of Death, and it is a magical creature, surely a bullet wouldn't stop it."

"Here we go again," said one of the cops from behind Jubilee. "Here we go again."

He wasn't the kind of man to believe in magic crap. Hell, he was barely the kind of man who believed in God, mother-hood, and apple pie. Lou DeMartino crossed his meaty forearms over his chest and wished he had an excuse to get the hell out of here.

Too many people, and he didn't like half of them. Okay, maybe more than half, since he hadn't even bothered to retain their names. He'd really been good at that shit once—introduce him to a roomful of people and he could cough back their names even out of order, making them all feel important.

These days, he didn't feel like making anyone feel important.

He didn't even feel important himself.

He leaned against the stupid wood paneling—if you could call that seventies crap wood—and wished he'd fixed the air conditioner last week when he'd been here, chatting up Izzy. He liked Izzy. She was no-nonsense, just as damaged as he was, and had some kind of darkness hiding behind her eyes.

Plus, she didn't judge. She knew he'd seen more than most, rejected more than most too, and had done his share of damage.

She didn't care. She would lightly touch his arm when she talked to him, smile at him without reservation (unlike the way she smiled at everyone else) and let him take his own sweet time to tell her why and how he'd found his own way here.

Everyone else assumed he'd seen something on the job, or it was some kind of accumulation of work and shootings and he let them think that. When Izzy asked her last-straw question, he'd never really answered it honestly, sometimes saying something facetious like *traffic stop*, which two of the African-Americans said, and they always looked at him or Frankie or Jose, the other cops, as if all three of them were responsible for whatever the hell other cops did all around America.

Only the African-Americans who said *traffic stop*, they never ever looked at the African-American cop, William something or other, because they never ever thought he'd be trigger happy, not at a traffic stop, not understanding that traffic stops were one of the most fraught things a cop could do.

You pull over a car, you don't know if it's a good citizen inside who will have their license and registration at the ready, who'll say *yes, officer,* and *no, officer,* and maybe, once everyone relaxed at little, might joke about having to pee or asking (sideways, maybe flirting) if they could get off with a warning this time.

You don't know if you got a good citizen or someone on

the run from something, someone with a gun on the passenger seat, someone who thinks the end is near and just fucking starts shooting, like they did to Lou's friend Ron five years ago. Ron survived, but he was on disability, *real* disability, not the psychiatric crap that Lou was on.

Not that Lou disagreed with his disability. It just wasn't the kind of thing a guy like him should have agreed to, something that a guy like him should've needed. He should've toughed it out, just like he was toughing these damn sessions out, with all the people pressed around him, the rattling air conditioner that dripped more water than it put into the air, the crap-ass carpet that didn't provide any protection for his thin ass against that solid (probably concrete) floor underneath.

If he'd known that the woman they'd come to vet, Lana something or other, would ask all the same stupid questions, express all the same stupid doubts, go through the same stupid discussion about magic and bullets and could they really have power over death—not that Biblical power over death crap, in which Jesus steps out of the tomb after three days and everyone prematurely declares death defeated, not that stuff—but a very real ability to fight Death or its minions or its angels or whatever the *fuck* you wanted to call it, on its own terms.

He didn't have time to listen to those questions again. Or rather, he did have time, he had all the time in the world, because he doubted he was ever going to get cleared, considering how jumpy he was, how much he hated being around other human beings, how just leaning against this wall, his butt pressed against the floor, Jubilee's mighty ass half a turn away from his face, how much all of that just made him want to crawl out of his skin.

But he didn't, not yet, although he might, if someone—anyone—doubted that magic existed one more time.

Jubilee turned just a little toward him, put one manicured finger to her beautifully painted lips, and nodded toward Rodrigo, who was listening to everything intently, as if she was saying, *Let Rodrigo handle it.*

If Rodrigo was going to handle it, he should've handled it before summoning everyone from their houses, from their all-important afternoon channel-surfing, watching the country implode because the president was a moron and, depending on which cable news channel Lou stopped on for which length of time, either the Democrats were at fault or the Republicans, and someone was going to get impeached or go to jail or should be left alone to do his goddamn job or maybe, maybe it was all broken, and they all needed to take a pill and lie down and hope that this too would pass.

Lou let out a long breath, and apparently, it had been really audible because half the room turned and looked at him.

"You got something to add, Lou?" Carter asked from across the room. Carter was one of the professors, someone who was used to asking snotty condescending questions, particularly at those whom he perceived as less educated and therefore less intelligent than he was.

"Yeah," Lou said, half-grunting the word as he stood up, so that he could tower over the sniper (although he would never tower over Jubilee, who was tall to begin with and always wore heels that made her at least six inches taller than she needed to be).

Lou pushed his way to the front of his little section of the group, looked at the sniper and thought, yep. She had sniper training all right. Probably not as good as she thought she was, but good enough for their purposes.

"Let me put it to you in really simple terms," he said to her, "so the rest of us don't have to listen to this shit for the umptiumpth millionth time. Magic exists. But it ain't really unusual, and that's where we all make the mistake. We justify off the magic stuff as every day—the way sunshine sparkles on water or the fact that a full moon brings out all the crazies worldwide—and we normalize much too much. Like death. We just figure, shit, yeah, it happens to all of us. Death and taxes, yadda yadda yadda."

The sniper—younger than he would've thought, eyes that weren't quite dead, not yet, but were heading there. She'd seen too much and she didn't want to believe in nothing. Jesus, he could understand that. He'd been in the same boat when he got here, right after Miriam died.

"We got it worked out," he said. "To answer your questions, maybe before you ask all of them, we're not gonna use regular bullets or silver bullets or bullets dipped in holy water. We ain't really using bullets at all. We got surprise on our side, and a whole hell of a lot of rage, and what you'd be shooting, from a distance and accurately—what a lot of us might be shooting, just not from that distance—are dummy bullets, maybe rubber, maybe non-lethal crowd control. We're going for shock and awe. You don't fight magic with magic when you're a bunch of lugs like us. You fight magic with sheer determination, a whole lotta righteousness, and the courage of our fucking convictions."

"And you think that'll work?" she asked.

Apparently, he'd missed that question in his little rant. He'd thought the answer was implied. Apparently not.

"Here's the thing you should understand, Miss Windspeed, Calculus, and Impossible Angles, you don't know if anything'll work until you give it a try. And conditions on the ground might make a great attempt fail. Or they might strengthen the weakest attempt ever designed. You know, luck. It can be a factor in anything we do."

"I thought you were going to tell me that luck is magic," she said.

He didn't know how she did it—found the one thing that would shut him down—but she did. Maybe that was magic.

He felt older than he had five minutes ago, just from the words she'd uttered. Stabbed him, right through the heart. Although there was an open track to that heart, and he knew it.

"I'm beginning to think luck is the antithesis of magic," he muttered, and shuffled back to his spot. Jubilee watched him. Damn, that woman saw everything. He used to too.

She gave him a compassionate look, half-hidden by her fake eyelashes, but there all the same, and turned back toward the sniper and her stupid questions.

Luck. Lou shook his head. Once upon a time, he'd thought of himself as the luckiest man alive. Whenever he introduced Miriam, he'd say, *She agreed to marry me. I think that makes me the luckiest man in the whole entire world.*

And then...Jesus... and then her cancer and all the magical medical crap in the world didn't save her. And she made him promise. Him, promise, that he would be the one, if she couldn't have a good life after the surgeries, if she was going to decline and become one-quarter of a person, if her life wasn't going to be worth living—she made him promise that he would have the docs pull the plug.

I trust you, she'd said. *You're the strongest man I know.*

But he wasn't strong. It came to that moment, when the

doctors said they couldn't make her better, they weren't even sure she would wake up from the last anesthetic, and if she did, they knew she wouldn't be herself because the freakin' cancer had eaten her beautiful brain.

He'd known that was coming, he'd *known* it when she looked at him—just the once, two weeks before—and for a half-second, she wondered who he was. She hadn't said that, thank God, because if she had, he might've wondered (ah, hell, he was still wondering) if he'd killed her because she didn't know him anymore.

But the docs talked to him, and then a whole other set of docs talked to him, and then yet another set of docs talked to him, and they all agreed that for all intents and purposes, for the purpose of the Do-Not-Resuscitate that she had signed, for the purpose of figuring out all the life and death stuff, she was already gone.

Already gone.

So he said, his voice choked with emotion, his voice barely there—the strongest man alive—he'd said, *Yeah. Do it. Pull the plug.*

And they did. They took her off life support. They let God do what God was going to do, as one of the docs said, and Lou damn near jumped down his throat.

Miriam didn't believe in God. She believed in logic and science and maybe some kind of something that humans hadn't discovered yet. She wasn't even sure there was life after death, which meant when she had told him that she wanted to die rather than live a marginal life, *she* had been the strongest person alive, because she believed that dying would probably wipe her out of existence entirely.

And she thought that was okay.

He didn't. He still didn't.

So he went from thinking he was the luckiest man alive to knowing that he was the unluckiest, because he had found the best person in the world, and then he had killed her.

Jubilee put her hand on his arm. Damn that woman, knowing and trying to alleviate other people's pain. Damn her for her compassion.

He wanted to move away.

Instead, he sniffled, and silently cursed himself, and if Jubilee hadn't been holding him down, he would've fled. He would've been done with this group.

No one looked at him, though. No one looked at sniveling former tough guys. No one, not even in this group, wanted to acknowledge that tears were possible and events in the world, in your goddamn life, could turn you into a weeping pile of worthlessness.

No one looked at him except Jubilee, and if she put one of her long arms around him, he silently swore he push her away. Hard. Noticeably hard.

He sniveled again, and wiped his nose with the back of his hand, and wished he could stop being such a goddamn baby.

Then he made himself concentrate, realizing he had lost the thread of the conversation.

"So you're saying we're going to be the Polish cavalry in World War II," the sniper was saying to the group.

Lou frowned, not knowing the reference. Jesus, his ignorance upset even him sometimes. Maybe instead of sitting on his ass and feeling sorry for himself every day, he should read a book once in a while.

"That's a myth," Carter said in his condescending tone. "The Polish did not attack German panzers with lances and swords. The Germans created myth as propaganda, and there you are, spouting it—"

Pauline, one of the few people Lou liked in the room, a teacher who had somehow survived Portage Elementary with the ability to smile and be nice even now, stepped in front of Carter just enough to shut him up.

"Yes," she said to the sniper woman. "That's exactly what we're saying. Sixteen times, the Polish cavalry faced stronger German forces, and in almost every one of those battles, the cavalry committed itself well. They succeeded at their missions. Yes, a lot of people died, but they died well and bravely, which is, I think, all we can hope for."

"Bullshit," the sniper said. She was shaking. "Bull-fuck-ing-shit. That well and bravely thing is something someone who has never been to war says because they believe that a hero's death is actually possible."

Oh, God, Lou thought. *Here it comes. The bile that no one in this place needs right now.*

And as if she had heard his thoughts, the sniper clenched her small fists.

"Well and bravely?" she asked. "You want a sniper. You know what a sniper sees through her scope? Someone living their life—maybe talking to a friend, maybe shooting at an enemy, maybe just crossing a road. We watch, we see, we put them in the crosshairs, and when the moment is right—when *we* determine that the moment is right—we shoot them."

The room was silent. Lou closed his eyes, wishing he could close his ears.

"They explode backwards as if propelled or maybe side-ways or maybe into the person they were talking to, and they don't get back up. They don't even try, if we're good, and those of us who do the job in war, we're good."

He sighed just a little and opened his eyes. He could shut his ears better with his eyes open. He stared at the open-toed shoes that Jubilee wore, her feet not pretty at all—very masculine, maybe the only masculine part about her. Except for the glitter toenail polish with the little stars in the very center, polish that matched her flowing pink outfit.

"They're not heroic. They're not brave. They were simply there one minute and gone the next. And everyone else? Yeah, maybe they have a moment where they grab a comrade and pull him aside or run in to carry out the wounded, but that doesn't negate what they did the day before, with their own rifle—"

"Enough," Rodrigo said quietly, the first words he had spoken in over an hour. "We know."

"You don't know," the sniper said. "You go on and on about being happy that you have a sniper, and you don't even know what we are—"

"We know," Lou said, before he could stop himself. "Jesus, woman, we know."

He didn't stand up this time. He sat there, the crown of his head leaning against the wall, his arms still crossed, his legs outstretched.

"You're the one who doesn't know," he said, as he pushed himself away from the wall. "You have no idea who we are or what we've been through. The person you're so rudely shouting down about heroism? That's Pauline, a school teacher—she's *still* a school teacher, although I don't know how, because I wouldn't be a school teacher after what she went through."

After all, he couldn't be a cop any more after what he

had gone through. At least not until they cleared him, not until he cleared himself.

"She saved the lives of fifteen six-year-olds, did you know that?"

"Lou," Pauline said, waving a hand, trying to make him stop.

"She took three bullets getting her first-grade class away from that crazy with an automatic weapon. You remember, the one who gunned down children because he wasn't properly potty-trained or whatever—"

"Lou," Pauline said, just a little louder.

"She's a hero. She made sure her kids were safe, then went back into the school and dragged out her colleagues. You see her. She makes you look like you're Arnold Schwarzenegger. If she had died that day, she would have died bravely and well—"

"Lou!" This time it wasn't Pauline. It was Izzy, and he realized what he had said. *If she had died that day.* God, where did these sentences come from?

He nodded, and would've shut up, if the sniper hadn't taken that moment to frown at him.

"You don't know us," he said. "You have no idea what we've been through, what we've seen, or why we're here."

"So why don't you tell me?" the sniper asked.

"Because, honey," he said, "people like you don't deserve to know."

And with that final insult, Lou DeMartino voted with his legs. He shot one last nasty look at Lana, then pushed his way past the people in front of him, and walked out the office door.

One by one, the others followed him. A number of them gave Rodrigo perplexed looks, as if they didn't know why he had brought them to the office in the middle of such a hot afternoon.

And he wasn't sure either, truth be told. He had seen her, saw the ghost of the rifle still in her hand, knew that she had been one of the best of the best, just by the aura around her, her eyes, and the way she still held that invisible gun.

But he couldn't see her soul. He couldn't see any of their souls. He could only guess and, as usual when he tried to lead, he guessed wrong.

He tried not to let despair take him. Self-pity was a waste of time. He firmly believed that, and yet, there he was, tottering on the edge of it.

Lana stood very still as the exodus began. She didn't

move as it continued, even as people around her left. Sometimes they brushed against her. Sometimes they bumped her so hard that she had to struggle to keep her footing.

Even when Rodrigo had brought in outspoken people like Lou DeMartino, the group had never reacted like this. They almost seemed to hate her.

Maybe they did hate her.

And that surprised him.

But she was the closest thing to a pure killer that he had tried to recruit for the team. There was clearly very little humanity left inside her.

And maybe that was good.

Only a handful of people were left. Izzy still sat at her desk. Jubilee stood near the wall, Tru beside her like they always were. Two of the police officers—William and Jose—and that professor, Carter, who grated on Rodrigo's nerves, even though Rodrigo knew the man's story. His entire extended family lost the day after he left for college, in a house fire that would have taken him too, had he been home. Day two of the family reunion. The day before he left for college, he'd had fifteen family members. Two days later, he had none.

He could've given up. Instead, he'd bottled up, and used his mind to move ahead, getting two Ph.D.'s and doing some post-doc work before getting snatched up by the university here. He was thirty-five before it all caught up to him, and even then, he hadn't understood it.

A friend had brought him to the grief group, and Rodrigo, seeing the anger underneath, had brought him here.

Lana's gaze met Rodrigo's as if to ask, *What now?*

He had no idea. The group had clearly rejected her, the

first time that had ever happened. Usually they accepted anyone he brought in.

Maybe they knew that with the arrival of a sniper, the plan would actually happen. Maybe that frightened them.

It was one thing to talk about killing the Angel of Death. It was another thing to actually try it.

He pushed away from the desk, feeling slightly chilled. The air conditioner failed when the room had been full, but now, its half-hearted wheeze managed to put out enough cold air to make him uncomfortable.

Or maybe, the fact that they had been close to executing his plan made him uncomfortable.

Because he had lied to all of them. He had never actually seen the Angel of Death.

He had felt the angel, over and over again. The beat of wings, the looming presence, that moment when the person, bleeding out in his arms, seemed to rally, only to smile, focus on something in the distance, and fade away.

Five tours. He hadn't lied about that. Five tours and lots of death, and that feeling just before someone left, that feeling he didn't know how to describe. When he'd been in the Arizona desert as a boy, crossing from Mexico with a group of people his mother had paid dearly for him to travel with, he could tell when someone wasn't going to make it.

Not because they gave any overt signs of illness or because they seemed to be on their last legs, but because the sun got very bright, and the air gained a chill it hadn't had before, and then the sound of flapping wings, not that he had known what that was the first time.

The first time, he had thought he heard sheets on a clothesline, flapping in the breeze, before he realized there was no breeze, no clothes line, no clean clothes.

And then the sun became so bright it hurt his eyes, and he shivered, and the next thing he knew, the slender man beside him, the one who had shared his water, the one who had egged him on, had fallen face first in the sand.

No matter what Rodrigo did—no matter what they all did—the slender man did not get up. He would never get up again.

The first of so many deaths. On that trip, another six succumbed. And then there were the people at the nursing home where he had gotten his first job. At that home, there was no sunlight. Just fluorescents that flared as if they were about to go out at the oddest hours. Only they didn't burn out. They stayed on, and didn't flare again, not until a few minutes before someone else died.

And then there were his tours. He didn't like to think about his tours. In fact, he couldn't think about them or the brilliant sunshine that seemed to coat everything. It couldn't get stronger there because it was already at full strength, something that sometimes made him wonder if he had actually served in a real place or if he had been doing his tours in a small corner of hell.

He wasn't sure; he had never been sure.

All he had done when he got home was try to find respite, try to figure out how to live with all he'd seen.

Which led him to the Meeting, and then the shooting, there.

He knew Izzy blamed him for some of the deaths, particularly young Alyssa. Because Izzy thought—maybe rightly—that he could have stopped it.

If he had seen it. If he hadn't been looking up, noting the chill on the breeze and the fact that the sun was brighter than he had seen it in years. And that surge of fear that had run through him—that had happened before the first gunshot, before Dugan had come out of the door, chasing everyone.

If Rodrigo had just looked down, he would have seen the movement in the glass panels beside the door, he would have known, he would have grabbed the rifle, saved lives.

He would have, he would have—if he had known, he wouldn't have taken the water from the man whose name he had never known. Rodrigo was younger, stronger, he could have made it through that desert on his own. And in the tours, he would have...

The air conditioner rattled, almost like the sound of flapping clothes on a line. He frowned, glanced at Izzy, who was staring in horror at Lana.

Lana, who had a handgun in her hand, her nearly dead eyes unfocused and unseeing.

Just like Dugan. Dear God, just like Dugan.

Rodrigo launched himself toward her as she raised that handgun slowly, aiming it—at him? He didn't have time to consider—and then the report echoed in the close quarters.

Out of the corner of his eye, he saw Jubilee grab Tru's neck and fling them to the ground as she went down. The police officers ran toward Lana, just like Rodrigo was doing, but Carter was staring toward the air conditioner itself.

The rattle had stopped, and the air inside the office had grown stifling.

Rodrigo reached Lana first. He tackled her, knocking her backwards, but she kept a grip on the handgun.

"Let me go, you fool," she said. "You want it dead, right? Let me make sure it's dead."

But he didn't let her go. He wasn't going to let anyone go. He had enough people die on his watch.

She was struggling beneath him.

"Let her go," Izzy said. "Rodrigo, let her go."

Jubilee was standing slowly. Tru stayed down, their head covered with their arms. The police officers were standing beneath the air conditioner, looking at the floor.

The air conditioner itself had changed color. A blackness covered it, almost an ichor—if that was the right word; it certainly wasn't one he had ever used before. The water from the broken condenser dripped down the wall, also black.

Izzy had stood, making her way around the desk.

"Let her go," Izzy repeated. "Before it vanishes. Let her go."

It. It. He didn't know what "it" was. He didn't see an it. But Jubilee was on her feet now, and Tru had let their hands slide from their skull.

He let Lana go, and she walked over to the desk, moving just beyond it, and poking with her toe.

Poking at nothing.

"Don't you see it?" Izzy asked.

"See what?" he asked.

"That shape over there," Carter said.

"The wings," said Jose.

"It's so small," William said.

"Andrew," Jubilee said.

"Alyssa," Izzy said.

"Alyssa?" It took Rodrigo a moment. The teenage girl, the one that Izzy had taken under her wing.

The one who had died at Dugan's hand.

Lana was still poking with her toe. "I didn't think a real bullet would kill it," she said.

Then she raised her head, her gaze meeting Rodrigo's. "You didn't see it?"

"I don't see anything," he said. He never saw anything. He should have told them that from the start. He never saw anything at all.

"The girl. Maybe twelve. She was—it was—" Lana shuddered. "It couldn't hide the wings. Or those eyes. All black, all pupil. No whites."

She looked at Izzy. "How long had she been coming here?"

Izzy was staring at the floor, in the space that Lana kept poking with her toe.

"I don't see a twelve-year-old," Izzy said. "It's Alyssa. Or it was, until…"

Jubilee walked toward them. "I should've known they could be hurt. The way that one ran from me after I punched it."

Rodrigo joined them. They were standing around something, only he couldn't see it. Nor could he see a bullet hole in the wall.

Just the ichor on the air conditioner, and a scent—something like rancid vanilla.

"What do we do with it?" Carter asked him, as if Rodrigo had all the answers. Although he probably deserved that. Because he always acted like he'd had answers.

"We can kill them?" he asked, astonished that it actually worked. Even though they hadn't tried.

"Yeah," Tru had joined the group. "Not that it matters. You all saw the other one, right?"

"No," Lana said. "I would have shot it too."

"You can't," Tru said. "They take lives at the right time. So if one is supposed to die…"

"Another shows up to make sure it does." Carter put a hand over his face, then staggered backwards just a little.

"It doesn't matter," William said. He normally didn't say much at all. "We sent a message. We let them know we're serious."

Lana looked at him sideways, as if to say, *You believe that?* Then she glanced at Rodrigo.

"It was here all along," she said. "Why didn't you just kill it?"

"I never saw it," he said, almost whispering. "I never saw any of them."

"Then why did you bring us here?" Izzy snapped, clearly furious. "Why did you promise us we could kill them? Why did you organize us? Why did you rent this office? Why did you—"

"Because," he said. "Some of us need more than talk. Some of us need to take action."

"Even if it's futile?" Izzy asked.

He had never seen her that angry.

"Especially if it is," he said.

He hadn't expected them to succeed. Expected one of them to succeed. Although he had known Lana was something special with her invisible rifle and her very real handgun, the one he hadn't realized she was carrying all along.

His gaze met hers, and there was something in her eyes, something livelier than there had been earlier in the day.

"It was feeding off you," she said. "Your pain. I was watching it. I saw the wings twice. And then, as everyone left—"

"The wings unfurled," Jubilee said. "I caught a glimpse of them."

"Was it coming for one of us?" Carter asked.

The bright light in the office. The chill. The sound of wings. Had that been for them? Or for the Angel of Death itself?

"How would we ever know?" Tru asked. "How would we ever know?"

No one wanted to leave. No one except Rodrigo.

They just kept staring at the dead creature that he couldn't see.

So finally, he walked out of the door, and sat on the cracked sidewalk, his feet extended in the ruined parking lot.

It was twilight. No more sunlight flaring. No bright day. No chill in the air. No wind. It was hotter than shit out here. Midwestern heat, filled with so much humidity that the air felt like a blanket, pressing down on him. Drowning him, with each breath.

But he kept breathing. Thinking.

He went to every Meeting. He came to this office every day. He talked about killing the Angel of Death, and then when it happened, when someone actually pulled it off, he felt as numb as he had in Afghanistan, when that last bomb exploded fifteen yards and two buildings away from where he was.

Triage was easy when you were numb. You didn't think

about the tattooed limbs as part of a man you'd spoken to not thirty minutes before. They were simply parts to be gathered, a job to be done.

That was what this had been for him.

A job.

A way to get through.

He crossed his arms over his knees and rested his forehead against his wrists. Magic had happened and he missed it. The event he had been planning for occurred. Ironically, the person he had brought in to do the job had done it, quickly, efficiently.

And, as he suspected, it had made no difference. Because there had been a second angel, there to take out the first.

Voices echoed behind him. Then laughter.

Laughter. When was the last time he heard laughter? Real joyous laughter?

He raised his head, saw Tru and Jubilee, smiling at each other as they came out of the building.

Jubilee crouched beside him. "It vanished on its own," she said. "Kinda like the witch in the *Wizard of Oz*."

"'Surrender, Dorothy!'" Tru quoted. "Guess threats like that never work."

"Judy's revenge," Jubilee said, and Tru laughed.

Tru started across the parking lot, but Jubilee stayed for a moment longer, crouching beside Rodrigo.

"What can I do for you?" she asked him.

He shook his head. He had no idea.

"It's nice to hear you laugh," he said. "Keep doing it."

She squeezed his shoulder, then stood. "You know where to find me."

"Yeah," he said, watching Tru shift from foot to foot in the parking lot. "Thanks."

Jubilee stood and headed to a car that Rodrigo hadn't seen before. More voices surrounded him. William, Jose, Carter, talking about what they had seen. They didn't acknowledge him, too intent on their conversation, perhaps, or maybe they hadn't seen him at all.

Then Lana. She sat down beside him, extended her legs and crossed them at the ankles.

"I suppose you want to hunt them," she said.

He let out a breath. Did he? Spend his entire life pursuing creatures he couldn't see? Being present at the worst moments, trying to figure out why the sun was brighter that day or the air had a chill? Did he really want to do any of that?

"No," he said. "You can, if you want."

"And be what?" she asked. "The Angel of Death for the Angel of Death? No thanks."

She wiped her hands on her thighs, as if her fingers had gotten dirty just from firing the gun.

"Your club is weird," she said. "I don't like it."

And he, he just realized, didn't like her. He let out a silent sigh, then got to his feet. He wondered if he should thank her.

But she made it easy. She just walked away from him, as if they hadn't spoken at all.

That just left Izzy. Izzy who was still inside the office. Izzy, who practically lived there.

He went inside and found her, sitting at her desk, staring at the apparently empty spot on the floor.

"What do we do now?" she asked, not looking at him. "What do we do now?"

He crouched in front of her, then leaned forward and

drew her into a hug. He'd known her nearly a year and he had never hugged her before.

She leaned against him, body stiff, and then, muscle by muscle, it relaxed.

It wasn't until his shoulder felt warm that he realized she was crying. He leaned his head against hers.

"Fucking wheel," she said after a few moments.

"Wheel?" he asked.

"Grief wheel," she said. "It's not a wheel. It's a gauge."

"A gauge?" He wasn't sure he understood what she was saying.

"Yeah," she said into his shirt. "Denial, anger, bargaining, depression, acceptance. It's not a wheel."

Bargaining. Jesus. The entire group had been built on bargaining. They had been negotiating how to kill the Angel of Death. Bargaining with the way the world worked, as if they could actually change it.

"I'd been stuck on anger," Izzy was saying.

And he had been bargaining. He'd brought them all into it.

"You're not stuck anymore?" he asked.

"I don't think I am." She brought her head up. Her cheeks were wet, and her eyes should have been red, but they weren't.

He wasn't stuck anymore either. But he felt a little lost, like he sometimes did when he finished a mission. Not that he had finished this one.

Or had he? He had finally found the right person, the catalyst, who changed everything.

What had Lou said? Their mistake... *We justify off the magic stuff as every day...we normalize much too much. Death and taxes.*

Death and taxes.

And Izzy, in his arms, warm and lighter than she had been since he met her.

She was watching him. He smoothed her hair away from her face. Then he kissed her. And she kissed him back.

Not hearts and flowers. Not even Disney-fied.

But nice. And different.

There was a reason he had relied on her, a reason he had trusted her.

They understood each other. They had needed each other. Right from moment one.

He helped her out of the chair.

"There's going to be a full moon tonight," he said, the king of non sequiturs.

"You saying we all went crazy because of it?" she asked.

He hadn't been. But he wouldn't put it past them. Any of them.

"Just thought maybe you'd want to see it," he said.

"I've already seen full moons," she said.

"But not this one," he said.

She stared at him for a moment. Then she smiled, nodded, almost laughed.

"You're right," she said. "Not this one. Chance of a lifetime."

It was. It was one of those moments—like every moment, really—that would never come again.

But he didn't say it.

Instead, he led her outside, to the ruined parking lot on a crappy street in a dying strip mall. A big orange moon was rising over the dilapidated buildings a few blocks away.

Orange meant there was a lot of sunlight reflecting off it. Big meant it was low on the horizon. And yet, it felt unusual. Magic. More magic than the actual magic that had occurred in their rundown office.

He put his arm around her, and she leaned into him. And they said nothing as the light hit them, brighter and brighter.

But the air stayed warm, and nothing flapped in the nonexistent breeze.

They were alone

They were together.

And, for that moment at least, they were alive.

SPIRIT GUIDES

KRISTINE KATHRYN
RUSCH

NEW YORK TIMES BESTSELLING AUTHOR

SPIRIT GUIDES

"KRISTINE KATHRYN RUSCH INTEGRATES THE FANTASTIC ELEMENTS
SO RIGOROUSLY INTO HER STORY THAT IT IS OFTEN HARD TO
REMEMBER SHE IS NOT MERELY RECORDING THE HERE AND NOW."
—*SCIENCE FICTION WEEKLY*

SPIRIT GUIDES

Los Angeles. City of the Angels.

Kincaid walked down Hollywood Boulevard, his feet stepping on gum-coated stars. Cars whooshed past him, horns honking, tourists gawking. The line outside Grauman's Chinese clutched purses against their sides, held windbreakers tightly over their arms. A hooker leaned against the barred display window of the corner drugstore, her make-up so thick it looked like a mask in the hot sun.

The shooting had left him shaken. The crazy had opened up inside a nearby Burger Joint, slaughtering four customers and three teenaged kids behind the counter before three men, passing on the street, rushed inside and grabbed him. Half a dozen shots had gone wild, leaving fist-sized holes in the drywall, shattering picture frames, and making one perfect circle in the center of the cardboard model for a bacon double cheeseburger.

He'd arrived two minutes too late, hearing the call on his police scanner on his way home, but unable to maneuver in traffic. Christ, some of those people who wouldn't let him pass might have had relatives in that Burger Joint. Still and all, he had arrived first to find the killer trussed up in a chair, the men hovering around him, women clutching sobbing children, blood and bodies mixing with French fries on the unswept floor.

A little girl, no more than three, had grabbed his sleeve and pointed at one of the bodies, long slender male and young, wearing a '49ers T-shirt, ripped jeans and Nikes, face a bloody mass of tissue, and said, "Make him better," in a whisper that broke Kincaid's heart. He cuffed the suspect, roped off the area, took names of witnesses before the back-up arrived. Three squads, fresh-faced uniformed officers, followed by the swat team, nearly five minutes too late, the forensic team and the ambulances not far behind.

Kincaid had lit a cigarette with shaking fingers and said, "All yours," before taking off into the sun-drenched crowded streets.

He stopped outside the Roosevelt, and peered into the plate glass. His own tennis shoes were stained red, and a long brown streak of drying blood marked his Levi's. The cigarette had burned to a coal between his nicotine-stained fingers, and he tossed it, stamping it out on the star of a celebrity whose name he didn't recognize.

Inside stood potted palms and faded glamour. Pictures of motion picture stars long dead lined the second floor balcony. Within the last ten years, the hotel's management had restored the Roosevelt to its 1920s glory, when it had been the site for the first-ever Academy Award celebration. When he first came to LA, he spent a lot of time in the hotel, imagining the low-cut dresses, the clink of champagne flutes, the scattered applause as the nominees were announced. Searching for a kind of beauty that existed only in celluloid, a product of light and shadows and nothing more.

El Pueblo de Nuestra Señora la Reina de los Angeles de Porciuncula.

The City of Our Lady, Queen of the Angels of Porciuncula.

He knew nothing of the Angels of Porciuncula, did not know why Felipe de Neve in 1781 named the city after them. He suspected it was some kind of prophecy, but he didn't know.

They had been fallen angels.

Of that he was sure.

He sighed, wiped the sweat from his forehead with a grimy hand, then returned to his car, knowing that home and sleep would elude him for one more night.

Lean and spare, Kincaid survived on cigarettes, coffee, chocolate and bourbon. Sometime in the last five years, he had allowed the LAPD to hire him, although he had no formal training. After a few odd run-ins and one overnight jail stay before it became clear that Kincaid wasn't anywhere near the crime scene, Kincaid had met Davis, his boss. Davis had the flat gaze of a man who had seen too much, and he knew, from the records and the evidence before him, that Kincaid was too precious to lose. He made Kincaid a plainclothes detective and never assigned him a partner.

Kincaid never told anyone what he did. Most of the cops he worked with never knew. All they cared about was that when Kincaid was on the job, suspects were found, cases were closed, and files were sealed. He worked quietly and he got results.

They didn't need him on this one. The perp was caught at the scene. All Kincaid had to do was write his report, then go home, toss the sneakers in the trash, soak the Levi's, and wait for another day.

But it wasn't that easy. He sat in his car, an olive green 1968 Olds with a fading pine-shaped air freshener hanging from the rearview mirror, long after his colleagues had left. His hands were still shaking, his nostrils still coated with the scent of blood and burgers, his ears clogged with the faint sobs of a pimply faced boy rocking over the body of a fallen co-worker. The images would stick, along with all of the others. His brain was reaching overload. Had been for a long time. But that little girl's voice, the plea in her tone, had been more than he could bear.

For twenty years, he had tried to escape, always ending up in a new town, with new problems. Shootings in Oklahoma parking lots, bombings in upstate New York, murders in restaurants and shopping malls and suburban family pick-ups. The violence surrounded him, and he was trapped.

Surely this time, they would let him get away.

A hooker knocked on the window of his car. He thought he could smell the sweat and perfume through the rolled-up glass. Her cleavage was mottled, her cheap elastic top revealing the top edge of brown nipple.

He shook his head, then turned the ignition and grabbed the gear shift on the column to take the car out of park. The Olds roared to life, and with it came the adrenalin rush, hormones tinged with panic. He pulled out of the parking space, past the hooker, down Hollywood Boulevard toward the first freeway intersection he could find.

Kincaid would disappear from the LAPD as mysteriously as he had arrived. He stopped long enough to pick up his clothes, his credit cards, and a hand-painted coffee mug a teenaged girl in Galveston had given him twenty years before, when she mistakenly thought he had saved her life.

He merged into the continuous LA rush hour traffic for the last time, radio off, clutching the wheel in white-knuckled tightness. He would go to Big Bear, up in the mountains, where there were no people, no crimes, nothing except himself and the wilderness.

He drove away from the angels.

Or so he hoped.

Kincaid drove until he realized he was on the road to Las Vegas. He pulled the Olds over, put on his hazards and bowed his head, unwilling to go any farther. But he knew, even if he didn't drive there, he would wake up in Vegas, his car in the lot outside. It had happened before.

He didn't remember taking the wrong turn, but he wasn't supposed to remember. They were just telling him that his work wasn't done, the work they had forced him to do ever since he was a young boy.

With a quick, vicious movement, he got out of the Olds and shook his fist at the star-filled desert sky. "I can't take it any more, do you hear me?"

But no shape flew across the moon, no angel wings brushed his cheek, no reply filled his heart. He could turn around, but the roads he drove would only lead him back to

Los Angeles, back to people, back to murders in which little girls stood in pools of blood. He knew what Los Angeles was like. Maybe they would allow him a few days rest in Vegas.

Las Vegas, the fertile plains, originally founded in the late 1700s like LA, only the settlement didn't become permanent until 1905 when the first lots were sold (and nearly flooded out 5 years later). He thought maybe the city's youth and brashness would be a tonic, but even as he drove into town, he felt the blood beneath the surface. Despair and hopelessness had come to every place in America. Only here it mingled with the cajing-jing of slot machines and the smell of money.

He wanted to stay in the MGM Grand, but the Olds wouldn't drive through the lot. He settled on a cheap tumble-down hotel on the far side of the strip, complete with chenille bedspreads and rattling window air conditioners that dripped water on the thin brown indoor-outdoor carpet. There he slept in the protective dark of the black-out curtains, and dreamed:

Angels floated above him, wings so long the tips brushed his face. As he watched, they tucked their wings around themselves and plummeted, eagle-like, to the ground below, banking when the concrete of a major superhighway rose in front of them. He was on the bed, watching, helpless, knowing that each time the long white tail feathers touched the earth, violence erupted somewhere it had never been before.

He started awake, coughing the deep racking cough of a three-pack-a-day man. His tongue was thick and tasted of bad coffee and nicotine. He reached for the end table, clicking on the brown glass bubble lamp, then grabbed his lighter and a cigarette from the pack resting on top of the cut-glass ashtray. His hands were still shaking, and the room was quiet except for his labored breathing. Only in the silence did he realize that his dream had been accompanied by the sound of the pimply faced boy, sobbing.

It happened just before dawn. A woman's scream, outside, cut off in mid-thrum, followed by a sickening thud and footsteps. He had known it would, the minute the car had refused to enter the Grand's parking lot. And he had to respond, whether it was his choice or not.

Kincaid paused long enough to pull on his pants, checking to make sure his wallet was in the back pocket. Then he grabbed his key and let himself out of the room.

His window overlooked the pool, a liver-shaped thing built in the late fifties of blue tile. The management left the terrace lights on all night, and Kincaid used those to guide him across the interior courtyard. In the half-light, he saw another shape running toward the pool, a pear-shaped man dressed in the too-tight uniform of a national rent-a-cop service. The air smelled of chlorine and the desert heat was still heavy despite the early morning hour. Leaves and dead bugs floated in the water, and the surrounding patio furniture was so dirty it took a moment for Kincaid to realize it was supposed to be white.

The rent-a-cop had already arrived on the scene, his pasty skin turning green as he looked down. Kincaid came up behind him, stopped, and stared.

The body was crumpled behind the removable diving board. One look at her blood-stained face, swollen and bruised neck, her chipped and broken fingernails and he knew.

All of it.

"I'd better call this in," the rent-a-cop said, and Kincaid shook his head, knowing that if he were alone with the body, he would end up spending the next few days in a Las Vegas lock-up.

"No, let me." He went back to his room, packed his meager possessions and set them by the door. Then he called 911 and reported the murder, slipping on a shirt before going back outside.

The rent-a-cop was wiping his mouth with the back of his hand. The air smelled of vomit. Kincaid said nothing. Together they waited for the Nevada authorities to show: a skinny plainclothes detective whose eyes were red-rimmed from lack of sleep and his female partner, busty and official in regulation blue.

While the partner radioed in, the rent-a-cop told his version: that he had been making his rounds and heard a couple arguing poolside. He was watching from the window when the man back-handed the woman, and then took off through the casino. The woman didn't get up, and the cop decided to check on her instead of chasing the guy. Kincaid had shown up a minute or two later from his room in the hotel.

The plainclothes man turned his flat gaze on Kincaid. Kincaid flashed his LAPD badge, then told the plainclothes man that the killer's name was Luther Hardy, that he'd killed her because her anger was the last straw in a day that had seen him lose most of their $10,000 savings on the Mirage's roulette table. Even as the men spoke, Hardy was sitting at the only open craps table in Circus Circus, betting $25 chips on the come line.

Then Kincaid waited for the disbelief, but the plainclothesman nodded, thanked him, rounded up the female partner and headed toward Circus Circus, leaving Kincaid, not the rent-a-cop, to guard the scene. Kincaid rubbed his nose with his thumb and forefinger, trying to stop a building headache, feeling the rent-a-cop's scrutiny. Kincaid could always pick them, the ones who had seen everything, the ones who had learned through hard experience and crazy knocks to check any lead that came their way. Like Davis. Only Kincaid was new to this plainclothesman, so there would be a hundred questions when they returned.

Questions Kincaid was too tired to answer.

He told the rent-a-cop his room number, then staggered back, picked up his things and checked out, figuring he would be halfway to Phoenix before they discovered he was gone for good. They would call LAPD, and Davis would realize that Kincaid had finally left, and would probably light a candle for him later that evening because he would know that Kincaid's singular talent was still controlling his life.

Like a hick tourist, Kincaid stopped on the Hoover Dam. At eight a.m., he stood on the miraculous concrete structure, staring at the raging blue of the Colorado below. An angel fluttered past him, then wrapped its wings around its torso and dove like a gull after prey. It disappeared in the glare of the sunlight against the water, and he strained, hoping and fearing he'd catch a glimpse as the angel rose, dripping, from the water.

The glimpses had haunted him since he was thirteen. He'd been in St. Patrick's Cathedral with his mother, and one of the stained glass angels left her window, floated through the air, and kissed him before alighting on the pulpit to tickle the visiting priest during Mass. The priest hadn't noticed the feathers brush his face and neck, but he had died the next day in a mugging outside the subway station at 63rd and Lexington.

Kincaid hadn't seen the mugging, but his train had arrived only a few seconds after the priest died.

Years later, Kincaid finally thought to wonder why he hadn't died from the angel's kiss. And, although he still didn't have the answer, he knew that his second sight came from that morning. All he needed to do was look at a body to know who had driven the spirit from it, and why. The snapshots remained in his mind in all their horror, surrounded by faces frozen in agony, each shot a sharp moment of pain that pierced a hole in his increasingly fragile soul.

As a young man, he believed he could stop the pain, that he had been given the gift so that he could end the horrors. He would ride out, like St. George, and defeat the dragon that had terrified the village. But these terrors were as old as time itself, and instead of stopping them, Kincaid could only observe them, and report what his inner eye had seen. He had thought, as he grew older, that using his skills to imprison the perpetrators would help, but the deaths continued, more each year, and the little girl in the Burger Joint had provided the final straw.

Make him better.

Kincaid didn't have that kind of magic.

The angel flew out of the wide crevice, past the canyon walls, its tail feathers dripping just as Kincaid had feared. Somewhere within a two-hundred-mile radius, someone would die violently because an angel had brushed the earth. Kincaid hunched himself against the bright morning, then turned and walked along the rock-strewn highway to his car. When he got inside, he kept the radio off so that the news of the atrocity would not hit him when it happened.

But the silence wouldn't keep him ignorant forever. He would turn on the TV in a hotel, or pass a row of newspapers outside a restaurant, and the information would present itself to him, as clearly and brightly as it always had, as if it were his responsibility, subject to his control.

The car led him into Phoenix. From the freeway, the city was a row of concrete lanes, marred by machine painted lines. From the side streets, it had well manicured lawns and tidy houses, too many strip restaurants and the ubiquitous mall. He was having a chimichanga in a neighborhood Garcia's when he watched the local news and realized that he might not hear of an atrocity after all. He finished the meal and left before the national news aired.

He was still in Phoenix at midnight, and had not yet found a hotel. He didn't want to sleep, didn't want to be led to the next place where someone would die. He was sitting alone at a small table in a high-class strip joint, sipping bourbon that actually had a smooth bite instead of the cheap stuff he normally got. The strippers were legion, all young, with tits high and firm and asses to match. Some had long lean legs and others were all torso. But none approached him, as if a sign were flashing above him, warning the women away. He drank until he could feel it—he didn't know how many drinks that was any more—and was startled that no one noticed him getting tight.

Even drunk, he couldn't relax, couldn't laugh. Enjoyment had leached out of him, decades ago.

When the angel appeared in front of him, he thought it was another stripper, taller than most, wrapped in gossamer wings. Then it unfolded the wings and extended them, gently, as if it were doing a slow-motion fan dance, and he realized that its face had no features, and its body was fat and nippleless like a butterfly.

He raised his glass to it. "You gonna kiss me again?" His thoughts had seemed clear, but the words came out slurred.

The angel said nothing—it probably couldn't speak since it had no mouth. It merely took the drink from him, and set the glass on the table. Then it grabbed his hand, pulled him to his feet, and led him from the room like a recalcitrant child. He vaguely wondered how he looked, stumbling alone through the maze of people, his right arm outstretched.

When the fresh air hit him, the bourbon backed up in his throat like bile. He staggered away from the beefy valets behind the potted cactus, and threw up, the angel standing beside him, still as a statue. After a moment, he stood up and wiped his mouth with the crumpled handkerchief he kept folded in his back pocket. He still felt drunk, but not as bloated.

Then the angel scooped him in its arms. Its body was soft and cold as if it contained no life at all. It cradled him like a baby, and they flew up until the city became a blaze of lights.

The wind ruffled his hair and woke him even more. He felt strangely calm, and he attributed that to the alcohol. Just as he was getting used to the oddness, the angel wrapped its wings around them and plummeted toward the ground.

They were moving so fast, he could feel the force of the air like a slap in his face. He was screaming—he could feel it, ripping at his throat—but he could hear nothing. They hurtled over the interstate. The cars were the size of ants before the angel extended its wings to ease their landing.

The angel tilted them upright, and they touched down in an empty, glass-strewn parking lot that led to an insurance office whose door was surrounded by yellow police tape. He recognized the site from the local newscast he had caught in Garcia's: ever since eight that morning, the insurance office had been the location of a hostage situation. A husband had decided to terrorize his wife who worked inside and, although shots had been fired, no one had been injured.

He stared at the building, felt the terror radiate from its walls as if it were a furnace. The insurance company was an old one: the gold lettering on the hand-painted window was chipped, and inside, he could barely make out the shape of an overturned chair. He turned to ask the angel why it had brought him there, when he realized it was gone.

Kincaid stood in the parking lot for a moment, one hand wrapped around his stomach, the other holding his throbbing head. They had flown for miles. He still had his wallet, but had no idea where he was or how he would find a pay phone.

And he didn't know what the angel had wanted from him.

He sighed and walked across the parking lot. The broken glass crunched beneath his shoes. His mouth was dry. The police tape looked too yellow in the glare of the streetlight. He stood on the stoop and peered inside, half hearing the voices from earlier in the day, the shouts from the police bullhorn, the low tense voice of the wife, the terse clipped tones of her husband. About noon he had gone outside to smoke a cigarette—his wife hated smoke—and had shot a stray dog to ward off the policeman who had been sneaking up behind him.

Kincaid could smell the death. He followed his nose to the side of the building. There, among the gravel and the spindly flowerless rose bushes, lay the dog on its side. It was scrawny and its coat was mottled. Its tongue protruded just a bit from its open mouth. Its glassy eyes seemed to follow Kincaid, and he wondered how the news had missed this, the sympathy story amidst all the horror.

The stations in LA would have covered it.

Poor dog. A stray in life, unremembered in death. Just standing over it, he could see the last moments—the enticing smell of food from the police cars suddenly mingled with the scent of human fear, the glittery eyes of the male human and then pain, sharp, deep, and complete.

Kincaid crouched beside it. In all his years, he had never touched a dead thing, never felt the cold lifeless body, never totally understood how a body could live and then not live within the same instant. In the past he had left the dead for someone else to clean up, but here no one would. The dog would rot in this site of trauma and near-human tragedy, and no one would take the care to bury the dead.

Perhaps that was why the angel brought him, to show him that there had been carnage after all.

He didn't know how to bury it. All he had were his hands. But he touched the soft soil of the rose garden, his wrist brushing the dog's tail as he did so.

The dog coughed and struggled to sit up.

Kincaid backed away so quickly he nearly fell. The dog choked, then coughed again, spraying blood all over the bushes, the gravel, and the concrete. It looked at him with a mixture of fear and pain.

"Jesus," Kincaid muttered.

He pushed himself forward, then grabbed the dog's shoulders. Its labored breathing eased and its tail thumped slightly against the ground. Something clattered against the pavement, and he saw the bullet, rolling away. The dog stood, whimpered, licked his hand, and then trotted off to fill its empty stomach.

Kincaid sat down in the glass and gravel, staring at his blood-covered hands.

Phoenix.

A creature of myth that rose from its own ashes to live again.

He had been such a fool.

All those years. All those lives.

Such a fool.

He looked up at the star-filled desert sky. The angel that had brought him hovered over him like a teacher waiting to see if the student understood the lecture. He couldn't relive his life, but maybe, just maybe, he could help one little girl who had spoken with the voice of angels.

Make him better.

"Take me to back to Los Angeles," he said to the angel. "To the people who died yesterday."

And in a heartbeat, he was back in the Burger Joint. The killer, an overweight acne-scarred man with empty eyes, was tied to a chair near the window, a group of men milling nervously around him, the gun leaning against the wall behind them. All the children were crying, their parents pressing the tiny faces against shoulders, trying to block the sight. The air smelled of burgers and fresh blood.

A little girl, no more than three, grabbed Kincaid's sleeve and pointed at one of the bodies, long slender male and young, wearing a '49ers T-shirt, ripped jeans and Nikes, face a bloody mass of tissue, and said, "Make him better," in a whisper that broke Kincaid's heart.

Kincaid crouched, hands shaking, wishing desperately for a cigarette, and grabbed the body by the arm. Air whistled from the lungs, and the blood bubbled in the remains of the face. As Kincaid watched, the face returned, the blood disappeared and a young man was staring at him with fear-filled eyes.

"You all right, friend?" Kincaid asked.

The man nodded and the little girl flung herself in his arms.

"Jesus," someone said behind him.

Kincaid shook his head. "It's amazing how bad injuries can look when someone's covered with blood."

He didn't wait for the response, just went to the next body and the next, his need for a cigarette decreasing with touch, the blood drying as if it had never been. When he got behind the counter, he gently pushed aside the pimply faced boy sobbing over the dead co-worker, and then he paused.

If he reversed this one, they would have nothing to indict the killer on.

The boy's breath hitched as he watched Kincaid. Kincaid turned and looked over his shoulder at the killer tied to the chair near the entrance. Holes the size of fists marred the drywall and made one perfect circle in the center of the cardboard model for a bacon-double cheeseburger. It would be enough.

He grabbed the body's shoulders, feeling the grease of the uniform beneath his fingers. The spirit slid back in as if it had never left, and the wounds sealed themselves as they would on a videotape run backwards.

All those years. All those wasted years.

"How did you do that?" the pimply faced boy asked, his face shiny with tears.

"He was only stunned," Kincaid said.

When he was done, he went outside to find the back-up team interviewing witnesses, the ambulances just arriving, five minutes too late.

"All yours," he said, before taking off into the sun-drenched crowded streets.

Now he had to keep moving. No jobs with police departments, no comfortable apartments. He had to stay one step ahead of a victim's shock, one step ahead of the press who would someday catch wind of his ability. He couldn't let them corner him, because the power was not his to control.

He was still trapped.

He stopped outside the Roosevelt, lit a cigarette, and peered into the plate glass. His own tennis shoes were stained red, and a long brown streak of drying blood marked his Levi's. The cigarette had burned to a coal between his nicotine stained fingers before he had a chance to take a drag, and he tossed it, stamping it out on the star of a celebrity whose name he didn't recognize.

All those years and he never knew. The kiss made some kind of cosmic sense. Even Satan, the head of the fallen angels, was once beloved of God. Even Satan must have felt remorse at the pain he caused. He would never be accepted back into the fold, but he might use his powers to repair some of the pain he caused. Only he wouldn't be able to alone, for each time he touched the earth, he would cause another death. What better to do, then, but to give healing power to a child, who would learn and grow into the role.

Kincaid's hands were still shaking. The blood had crusted beneath his fingernails.

"I never asked for this!" he shouted, and people didn't even turn as they passed on the street. Shouting crazies were common in Hollywood. He held his hands to the sky. "I never asked for this!"

Above him, angels flew like eagles, soaring and dipping and diving, never coming close enough to endanger the Earth. Their featureless faces radiated a kind of joy. And, although he would never admit it, he felt that joy too.

Although he would not slay the dragon, he wouldn't have to live with its carnage either. Finally, at last, he could make some kind of difference. He let his hands fall to his side, and wondered if the Roosevelt would shirk at letting him wash the blood off inside. He was about to ask when a stray dog pushed its muzzle against his thigh.

"Ah, hell," he said, looking down and recognizing the mottled fur, the wary yet trusting eyes. He glanced up, saw one angel hovering. A gift then, for finally understanding.

He touched the dog on the back of its neck, and led it to the Olds. The dog jumped inside as if it knew the car. Kincaid sat for a moment, resting his shaking hands against the steering column.

A hooker knocked on the window. He thought he could smell the sweat and perfume through the rolled up glass. Her cleavage was mottled, her cheap elastic top revealing the top edge of brown nipple.

He shook his head, then turned the ignition and grabbed the gearshift on the column to take the car out of park. The dog barked once, and he grinned at it, before driving home to get his things. This time he wouldn't try Big Bear. This time he would go wherever the spirit led him.

New York Times bestselling author Kristine Kathryn Rusch writes in almost every genre. Generally, she uses her real name (Rusch) for most of her writing. Under that name, she publishes bestselling science fiction and fantasy, award-winning mysteries, acclaimed mainstream fiction, controversial nonfiction, and the occasional romance. Her novels have made bestseller lists around the world and her short fiction has appeared in eighteen best of the year collections. She has won more than twenty-five awards for her fiction, including the Hugo, *Le Prix Imaginales*, the *Asimov's* Readers Choice award, and the *Ellery Queen Mystery Magazine* Readers Choice Award.

Publications from *The Chicago Tribune* to *Booklist* have included her Kris Nelscott mystery novels in their top-ten-best mystery novels of the year. The Nelscott books have received nominations for almost every award in the mystery field, including the best novel Edgar Award, and the Shamus Award.

She writes goofy romance novels as award-winner Kristine Grayson.

She also edits. Beginning with work at the innovative publishing company, Pulphouse, followed by her award-winning tenure at *The Magazine of Fantasy & Science Fiction*, she took fifteen years off before returning to editing with the original anthology series *Fiction River*, published by

WMG Publishing. She acts as series editor with her husband, writer Dean Wesley Smith, and edits at least two anthologies in the series per year on her own.

To keep up with everything she does, go to kriswrites.com and sign up for her newsletter. To track her many pen names and series, see their individual websites (krisnelscott.com, kristinegrayson.com, retrievalartist.com, divingintothewreck.com, pulphousemagazine.com).

kriswrites.com